AF706201

Zindagi Ek Ehsaas

Flairs and Glairs

Publication House

"Zindagi Ke Ehsaas"

ISBN No: " 978-93-90416-26-4"
1st Edition
Language – English and Hindi

Flairs and Glairs
Publication House
Regd. Under MSME Act.

Disclaimer

This anthology is entirely a work of fiction. The compiler has done her best to testify the originality of the content of all the authors and checked for possibilities of plagiarism. All the write-ups are unique and published only in this book.

If any plagiarism and/error is found, it will solely be the responsibility of the co-author, and not the compiler or publisher.

The opinions expressed in the anthology are only of the co-authors and not of the compiler or publisher

Co Author

1. Shubham Shah (Founder Flairs and Glairs)
2. Akanksha Sinha (Compiler)
3. Ishani Agarwal
4. Ishika Agarwal
5. Koel
6. Prashant Bajpai
7. Sandhya Rani Mishra
8. Swetapadma Nanda
9. Gargi Kharbanda
10. Anushka Kesarwani
11. Deepti Sharma
12. Jatin Senapati
13. Anuradha Chakrawarti
14. Naveen Shukla
15. Sarita Gawde
16. रक्षा गुप्ता
17. Feroz Ahmad Dar
18. Piyush Kumar
19. Palak Inwati
20. Lalitha Srinivas
21. Shreya Vij
22. Rajan V Kokkuri
23. Kavita Misra
24. Atul Yadav
25. Anzar Usmani
26. Monika Goswami
27. Sayani Bag
28. Keerthi Ravishankar
29. Sonali Joshi
30. Gayatri Gor

31. Ayushi Bhatnagar
32. Shipra S Gupta
33. Sakshi Singh
34. Nishant Kamble
35. Richa Rohit Gupta
36. Sakshi Sehrawat
37. Bhagyasree. G
38. Aysha Nihidha
39. Annu Singh
40. Ritwika Ghosh
41. Pradeep Sengar
42. Anupama Das
43. Abhilash Rout
44. Asmita Bansod
45. Reshma Bhattacharyya
46. Aysha Afrin K M
47. Abirami B V
48. Dr Sayanee Saha
49. Gaayathri Maya
50. Ruchi Vachhani
51. Saheli Banerjee
52. Shreyansh Shreshth
53. Aditi Palmate
54. Amruta Makode
55. Dr. Rwitu Ghosh
56. Diya Mehta
57. Avnish Kumar
58. Shilpa Sahu
59. Saira Siddiqui
60. Sanchana Jayakumar
61. Khanida Firdose M
62. Master Piyush Kranti
63. Saloni Lal Srivastava

64. Ashish Kumar Singh
65. Hermit
66. Moitry Das
67. Yash Raj
68. Suman
69. Shubham Raj
70. Dr.Binayak Bibek Das
71. Alok Abhishek
72. Mitali Madhusmita Das
73. Pratibha Kumari
74. Himmat Singh Johal
75. Richa Tirthani
76. Mihir Raghuwanshi
77. Jyoti Duggal
78. Vivek Maurya "Sarkar"
79. Srishti Upneja
80. Govind M Waswani
81. Monika
82. Nicky Bharat
83. Samiksha
84. Mariya Suryavanshi
85. Samiran Bhatt
86. Ananya Kumar
87. Ankita Hundekar
88. Sanamsmita Sahu
89. Ashutosh Kumar
90. Anjali Singh
91. प्रांसूर्य भटट्
92. Kiran Gehlot (Siya)
93. Kritika Sharma
94. Sourabh Sinoy
95. Gurdeep Kaur
96. Akash Malhotra

97. Sana Tabassum
98. Neeha Muneer
99. Roopali Purohit
100. Smruti Paik
101. Himani Raheja
102. Ishita Kesarwani
103. Jagdish
104. Utkarsha Bhosale
105. Asha Paul

Shubham Shah

(Founder- Flairs and Glairs and Compiler)

Shubham Shah, entrepreneur at "Flairs & Glairs" a brand with dynamics in events organizing and cultural educational pan INDIA, He is a 26yr. old guy who recently has entered, the digital platform of imprinting emotions. He has initiated with his own open mic platform to help budding poets and aspiring writers under his brand named as "Teekhe Zasbaaat"
He is a commerce graduate from Bhagalpur City of Bihar.
He says Writing has impersonated him since childhood and he has now been writing for over a decade!

Cooking, on the other hand, is his passion! He also mentions, trying out new things just tickles him!
When asked sir, Why SPICY EMOTIONS?
He smiled and added, "agar jasbaat teekhe na ho toh wo jasbaat kaha" Spices are all that blends! So do his words!
As a chef, he presents to you his dish! Hot and freshly served! Taste it! Feel it! Enjoy it! You can also find his writing in the Solo book "Teekhe Zasbaaat" and 70+ anthologies. With his passion to explore opportunities across Platforms he is working with keen devotion and We wish him all the very best for his future ventures
Share your reviews on his

INSTAGRAM

@spicy_emotions
@shubham4shah

Or via email on

shubham2shah@gmail.com

To stay tuned to his work and opportunities follow his business Handles

INSTAGRAM FACEBOOK YOUTUBE

@flairsandglairs
@teekhezasbaaat

WEBSITE:

https://flairsandglairs.in/
https://flairsandglairs.com/

Zindagi Ke Ehsaas

Ehsaas E Zindagi Tumko Sunate
Tum Jo Dur Jate Tumhe Paas Buate
O Suno Ji Kehkar Tumhe Bulate
Han
Tum Jo Dur Jate Tumhe Paas Buate
Tham Kar Tumhara Hath Tumhe Kareeb Late…

Samajh Nahi Aata Tumhe Kya Kya Kse Kse Samjhate…
Kse Btate
Ho Kitne Zaruri Iska Ehsaas Dilate
Ki Yu Toh Zindagi Bohot Labi Hai
Ya Hum Kaat Le Ya Jee Le

Kaati Bohot Hai Zindagi Tumhare Bina Ab Tumhare Sath Jeena Cahte Hai
Ehsaas E Zindagi Kya Hai Tumhe Btana Cahte Hai…
Ab Tumhare Sath Chala Cahte Hai…
Har Pal Me Ab Khushiyan Batorna Cahte Hai…
Tumhare Sath Chalna Cahte Hai…
Riste Ko Mukaam Tak Pahuchana Cahte Hai…
Tumhare Sath Ek Aasiyan Bnana Cahte Hai…

Akanksha Sinha

(Compiler)

Akanksha Sinha is student by profession ,writer as passion. Lives in Patna,Bihar. She loves to portrait feelings by her poetry and quotes,she likes travelling and capturing moments. Heart healer by birth. She is co author of 15+ anthology. She loves to feel the nature. She is passionate &ambitious for her work.

Currently, she is been a co-author in several anthologies and compiling her first anthology named ""Zindagi-Ek-Ehsaas""...

She has own page namely "" @merelabzz "" on Instagram.

ज़िन्दगी से बहुत उदास हूँ

न जाने क्या क्या मैं भी सोचती रहती हूँ
कभी इधर तो कभी उधर देखती रहती हूँ
कुछ लोग कहते हैं कि मैं बहुत खास हूँ
मगर कौन बताए कि मैं जिंदगी से बहुत उदास हूँ

कुछ पल तो ऐसा लगता है कि कुछ हो रहा हो
कभी दिल तो कभी दिमाग भी कुछ कह रहा हो
महसूस होता है जैसे मैं किसी के आसपास हूँ
पर मैं तो जिंदगी से बहुत उदास हूँ

कोई तो है जो बेइन्तहा मुझसे प्यार करता है
मेरे आने का हर वक्त वो इंतज़ार करता है
उसे कौन बताए कि मैं बकवास हूँ
क्योंकि मैं तो जिंदगी से बहुत उदास हूँ

कहता है कि मैं कभी भी हार नहीं सकती
मगर मैं तो जीत कर भी जीत नहीं सकती
वो कहता फिरता है सब से मैं विश्वास हूँ
न जाने क्यों मैं जिंदगी से बहुत उदास हूँ

सब कुछ जान कर भी अनजान बनी रहती हूँ
मैं तो अपने ही घर मे मेहमान बना रहती हूँ
घर वाले कहते है की मैं एक उपन्यास हूँ
बे-वजह ही मैं जिंदगी से बहुत उदास हूँ ।।"

दास्ताने ज़िन्दगी

ज़िन्दगी को जितना समझना चाहती हूँ मैं,
ज़िन्दगी मुझे उतना ही उलझा देती है।

ज़िन्दगी से जितना भागती हूँ मैं,
ज़िन्दगी मेरे उतने ही पास आ जाती है।

ज़िन्दगी को जितना ही भूलना चाहती हूँ मैं,
ज़िन्दगी मुझे उतना ही रुला जाती हैं।

ज़िन्दगी को जितना ही जीना चाहती हूँ मैं,
ज़िन्दगी मुझे उतने ही बेरहमी से मार जाती है।

हर वो चीज जो मैं पाना चाहती हूँ,
ज़िन्दगी मुझसे छीन ले जाती है।

जिंदगी को मैं जब भी जीतना चाहती हूँ,
जिंदगी मुझे सफाई से हरा जाती है।

जब कभी मैं दिल खोल के रोना चाहती हूँ,
ये कंबख़्त ज़िन्दगी आँसू तक बहाने नहीं देती हैं।

ज़िन्दगी में जब भी मरना चाहती हूँ मैं,
ज़िन्दगी मुझे उस पल ही जीना सीखा जाती हैं।"

अनमोल रिश्ते

कुछ अनजाने रिश्ते बड़े अनमोल होते है,
कोई मोल नहीं होता उनका वो बेमोल होते है ।
ना कोई अधिकार न स्वाभिमान होता है,
कड़वाहट नहीं होती बस मीठी बोल होते है

उम्मीद होती नहीं इन रिश्तों में
दूर रहकर भी निभाते, बेजोड़ रोल होते है
अपनापन नहीं मिलता कभी कभी अपनो से
तब ये रिश्तें निभाते अहम रोल होते है

छीन लेते है अपने ही कुछ खास हमारी मुस्कान
तो कुछ रिश्ते दिल के बन्द पन्ने, रहे खोल होते है
बिन कहे भी पहचान लेते है वो हमारी तकलीफ
तो वही कुछ अपने हमारे दिल को, रहे तोल होते है

पैसों के तराजू पर अब तुल रहे है रिश्ते
पर कुछ अनकहे रिश्ते जीवन में बेमोल होते है
हो सके तो सम्भाल कर रखना इन रिश्तो को
छल कपट नकाब की दुनिया में वो अनमोल होते है ।।"

ज़िन्दगी तुझसे सवाल बहुत है

ज़िन्दगी तुझसे सवाल बहुत है
तेरे नखरे भी कमाल बहुत है
कभी फुर्सत से मुझसे मिल तू
बैठ के साथ मेरे, मुझसे बात कर तू

सुना है तु बड़ी खामोश रहती है
अपनी शातिर निगाहों से मुझपर नजर रखती है
कब तक ऐसे लुका छिपी करती रहेगी जानती सब है पर तु कुछ न कहेगी
न जाने किस पल का इंतजार है तुझे
ना जाने कौन सी घड़ी में आना होगा तेरा ?
कभी कभी ख्याल आता है तुझसे रूठी रहूं और खामोश हो जाऊं ,
तू मनाने आए और मैं फ़िर मान जाऊं, बैठकर हम फिर सारी बातें करेंगे
रात दिन बस हंसते मुस्कुराते रहेंगे,

फिर न ही किसी का इंतजार होगा
तेरी मेरे दरमियां किसी के लिए न कोई जगह होगी,
मुद्दतों बाद मैं मन ही मन खिल-खिलाऊँगी,
तुम हमको और मैं तुमको अपनी कहानी सुनाऊँगी।
ऐ जिन्दगी तुझसे शिकायत तो बहुत है
कभी पास आकर तु बैठ तो सही
मेरा तुझसे सवाल बहुत है ।

Ishani Agarwal

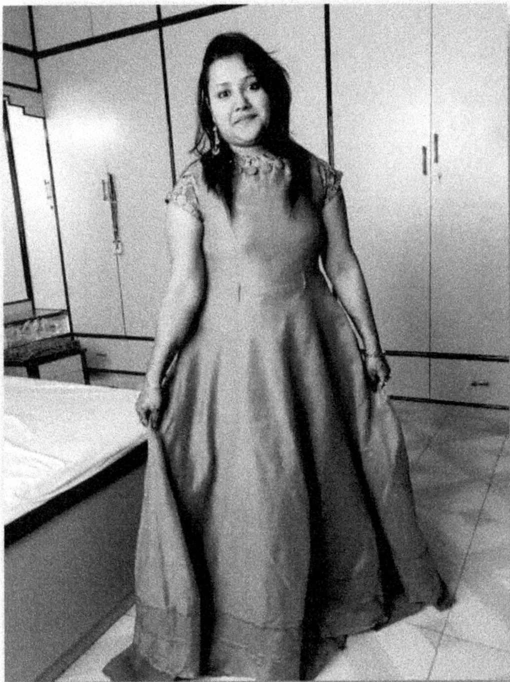

Ishani Agarwal
Born and brought up in Kolkata, she has done her schooling and college from here itself. She is doing her post-graduation at the moment. Ishani loves talking to people around, and is excited for this new beginning of hers! Been a Compiler for 35+ Anthologies, and in the process for more, also, co-authored in 100+ Anthologies, Ishani is very Happy with how her life is turning out now!
Insta handle: Ishani_agarwal_quotes

(1)

Life is a Rollercoaster

Not at the best of Life,
But not at the worst either...
Life is a Rollercoaster in itself,
And I am just riding along...
Somewhat fun,
Somewhat scary,
Somewhat sad,
Somewhat happy...
Don't know which emotion overtakes which one,
And when !
This Journey is hopefully long...
Let's see where I end up in the end !

Ishika Agarwal

Ishika is a 16 years old girl.
Writing for her is nothing else but a passion. She hails from the city of Joy and Art. She has been a Co-author in 30+ anthologies in the recent past, all adding on experiences to her. Been a part of India book of Record projects like Black and World Record projects like 15 wonders of Poetry, Ishika is paving her way to success.

(1)

What is the feeling of life? People ask.
I say feeling is life.
If we didn't feel anything then there would be no experiences.
No bad or happy memories.
There wouldn't be pain or relief.
There wouldn't be ignorance or hatred or even ego.
But most importantly love wouldn't be there.
Love is a feeling that expresses all other emotions.
I would say again feeling is life.

Koel

Koel is belongs from W.B. and currently residing in Mumbai. She's a 18 year old singer, narratior and poet. Poetry is a form of art where vocabulary aligns in such a beautiful way that it express emotions like never before according to her. .

Timless

Timeless was her efforts and dreams
Caused many scars and screams
Life bestowed many shades on her
She stood firm and dream of many she is now."

Life's Games

Scrabbled up my fate, doddled up destiny.
Showered providence for a while, showered imprudence in next
Life loves adventurous games I guess,
And composes savage role plays as well.
I've awaited a lot, but now I know you take your turn here not wait for it."

Flips

When I was going well life flipped on tombs
When I was used to tombs life flipped on glory
When bunch of glory came to me life flipped again
Then I become an ""object"" to scron.
Guess what, life kept flipping and I learnt parkour. "

Prashant Bajpai

His name is Prashant Bajpai. He lives in Lucknow. He is having graduate B.A(English). He is having a great writing skill. He is a person with great character. Writing ideas are always in his mind. He runs the page @feelingsgotowords on instagram.

तेरे जाने के बाद

तेरे जाने के बाद कुछ ,
खोया खोया सा रहता हूं,
खुद से खफा खफा सा रहता हूं,
तेरा जाना मेरी जान जाने जैसा है,
काश कुछ ऐसा हो तूझे रोक लू,
अपने पास हमेशा के लिए और कभी ना जाने दू,
क्योंकि तेरे जाने से मै अधूरा सा रहता हूं,
इसलिए खुद से खफा खफा सा रहता हूं।।

यूं नजरंदाज ना कर तू मुझे,
कुछ लफ्ज़ दो लफ्ज़ बात कर,
मै तेरा हूं ये तू भी जानती है,
तो फिर यूं परेशान ना कर।।

तेरी यादें

तुझसे मुलाकात की यादें,
जब भी याद आती है मुझको,
मै कुछ दिन तक खोया सा रहता हूं,
और एक ऐसी निशानी दी खुदा तूने,
चेहरे से मुस्कुराता तो हूं ,
पर अखो से गीला रहता हूं।।

हर शाम याद आ जाती हो तुम,
मेरे खयालों में छा जाती हो तुम,
ख़्वाबों में बात करने की कोशिश करता हूं,
बहुत याद आ जाती हो तुम।।

तेरा ज़िक्र

मेरे ख्वाबों में जब भी तेरा ज़िक्र आता है,
कसम से मेरी नींद उड़ा ले जाता है,
तुम चाहती हो हम तुम्हे भूल जाए,
तुम तो जान हो मेरी,
जान को कैसे भूल सकता है कोई।।

आज फिर उससे ख्वाबों में मुलाकात हुई,
बैठ कर उससे कुछ मेरी बात हुई,
मै सोचता रहा काश रात ऐसे चलती रहे,
और ऐसे ही तुझसे मिलता रहूं,
और खूब सारी बातें करता रहूं।।

माना थी कुछ मजबूरिया

माना थी कुछ मजबूरियां,
हम दोनों को अलग कर गई,
पर दूर करके भी तुझे मेरे पास कर गई,
सच्चा प्यार बिछड़ने पर भी अलग नहीं होता,
ये उसको हम समझा ना पाए,
समझाते समझाते चूर चूर हो गए हम,
इसलिए हालातो से मजबूर हो गए हम,
वो कहती है भूल जाओ अच्छा है,
प्यार है या खिलवाड़ दिल से,
कोई सच्चा प्यार भूल सकता है।।

उस बात छिपाने का हुनर आता था,
पर मुझे सब पता चल जाता था,
मैंने उससे प्यार किया था सच्चा वाला,
उसने क्या किया ये वो ही जानता था।।

Sandhya Rani Mishra

"Sandhya Rani Mishra a research scholar belonging to koraput (odisha). She is a learner love to observe different behaviour of people and explore the world surrounding her, and always try to grab something new and implementation of these things in her day to day life. Otherwise she completed her master's in chemistry from NIST, Berhampur,odisha. Now she is persuing her PhD. In NIT Rourkela. However she is a story teller, motivational speaker and love-break up quote writer. She write her experience and observations and love to live her words and always try to learn new lessions from the society.

जिंदगी

जिन्दगी फिर मुस्कुराने लगी,
थोड़ा , ठहरी और इतराने लगी,
लोग जिससे आसुं समझ रहे थे,
नमक का पानी सोच पीने लगी,
उसने मुड़ कर देख क्या लिया,
ये तो उछल उछल के नाचने लगी।
उसका तसवीर अपने आखों में
लेकर घूमती है, कोई देखना ले,
इसलिए नजर कभी नहीं उठती है।
उसका जिक्र जहां होता है
वहीं ठहर जाती है,
थोड़ा मुस्कुराती है ,और थोड़ा रोती है,
पड़ोस में ही रहती है, जब भी मिलती है,
नजरे कम और हात ज्यादा मिलती है,
उस से मिल,दिल में फिरसे अरमान जगने लगी,
थोड़ा ठहरी और गुनगुनाने लगी।
जिन्दगी फिर मुस्कुराने लगी।

मुहब्बत है

एक बार ही कह दो
कितना मुहब्बत है।
एक बार ही दिखा दो
कितना चाहत है।
ना दिन ढले,ना ढलती राते हें,
एक बार ही कह दो,
तुम्हें मेरी जरूरत है।
डरों मत, दोस्ती नहीं तोड़ेंगे,
जितना है ,अब ज्यादा गहरा बनादेंगे,
सुनो, कह दोना,
मेरे होनेसे ,तुमको कितना राहत है।
कितना कुछ सोच कर आते हो,
मुझे देख क्यू चुप हो जाते हो,
देखा है मेने छीप छिप कर रोते हो,
आरे, एक बार कह क्यू नही देते हो,
मेरा प्यार ही तेरा इबादत है।
मेरा गुस्सा हो या खुशियां,
हसी ख़ुशी सब झेल लेते हो,
पर एक बार भी ,
उदास होने नहीं देते हो,
कह दोना, तु मेरी रुकसत है,
कह दोना तुम मेरी मुहब्बत है।

आसुं

एक बारिश जो रोज आती है,
दिलसे हो कर रूह तक जाती है,
थोड़ा नमकीन, थोड़ा गरम होती है,
बिन बादल बरसती रहती है।
खुशियां, हो या गम इस को आना ही है,
वरना कोई जज़्बात रंग ना लाती है,
बिन धारा ये बहती रहती है,
जितना छिपाओ सबको दिख जाती है।
बिन जुबां सब बोल जाती है,
कभी दिल हल्का कर देती है,
कभी आखें भर देती है,
लाखों वजह की रानी है,
पर कहती सबकी काहानी है।
आसमान से नहीं टपकती है,
फिर भी बरसती रहती है,
बिजली इसकी साथी नहीं,
फिर भी चमकती रहती है,
मौसम की कोई परवाह नहीं,
इसकी आना है आजाती है।
बरसात भिगाए हमे,
ये तोह तकिया भीगती है,
जितना भी दर्द हो, थोड़ा
निकल कर सुकून देती है।
कभी ठंडी, कभी थोड़ा गरम होती है,
ये जो बिन मौसाम बरसात हेन,
आखिर कार ""आसू "" कह लाती है।"

तेरी याद

तेरी याद आती है ,
आखों में आंसू दिल में गम दे जाती है,
फिर भी तेरी याद आती है।
जख्म वो, मरहम वोही बन जाती है,
एक पहर खत्म अब दूसरी आजाती है,
कमवक़्त तेरी याद रुला जाती है।
फिर भी तेरी याद आती है।
वो साल, वो घड़ी , सब बीत गए,
अब आंखों से अश्रु के धारा बह जाती है,
सुप्त, घाव को जगा जाती है,
यकीनन तेरी याद आती है।
मेहरूम, मरहम बन ,
आग लगा जाती है,
लाखों खयाल दबा कर बाहर आ जाती है।
हां तेरी याद आती है।
दिल से हो कर जो आखों में छलक ती है,
सावन में बारिश के साथ बह जाती है,
हां तेरी याद आती है ।
गुम सुम, गुम सूम, चुप चुप,
घर के कोने में, बिस्तर के ऊपर,
जो आहें निकलती है।
हां तेरी याद आती है।
सबसे छिपाए तेरा चेहरा,
जो रोज ,मख्खी का बहाना देती है।
हां तेरी याद आती है।

Swetapadma Nanda

Swetapadma Nanda is a young and upcoming poet, an avid reader and author of _. All of 23 years, she has a degree in Journalism from Madras Christian College and lives in Nagpur, with a penchant for poetry and has a published anthology (_) and several featured works to her name. Her poetry shines light on love, life and everything in between.

Little Do You Know

It was one of the pages that I would keep it safe , the words scribbled in frustrations and anger . Reflections of losses and heart breaks . The words was buried of utter sadness and fears . Little do they know it turned out to be chants of cheers . Indeed it was a phase awake of reality ,
Those times helped me to be brave and strong and make headway to glory .
They say life is struggle ,
Little do they know it's a stage of cocoon ,
Creating beautiful creatures like butterfly .
Have patience and wait for the change ,
Let the pages of yours turn over again.
Filled with adventures and joyous reign .
No matter how many people stayed and chose to walk off ,
I chose to leave my past behind and takeoff.
Little do they know inspite of shortcoming and failures,
Wait and watch my moves , it was just the trailer ."

Gargi Kharbanda

"She writes to explore herself and to calm and glorify the person hidden inside her. She writes to express her immense thoughts which may relates to one another and binds with the strands of love, emotions, understanding and pain.
Through her writeups
She intend to narrate her unspoken story which is embraced by the most.
She express her hidden self in the form of writing."

Puberty

Puberty hits hard,
Those painful pimples leaving their imprints on our body .
Makes us forget about our favorite show "Noddy"".
Those first menstrual stain in class leaving us embarrassed.
Memories of childhood now cherished...
That hairy growth on pubic regions,
Makes a down fall of hair from our scalp.
Whole system is on fire yet no one to help.
Beauty of a girl before puberty is measured from her face.
And after puberty hits body is new measuring tape.
Puberty makes our world shoddy.
We are mature enough to understand things
Yet we are still small kids.
Group of girls talking about boys
Boys talking about curls of girls
That never happened before
Which means puberty now hits till the core.
Boys want their body to be giant,
Where as girls want it to be slim with glam.
Stage of puberty comes for a reason
And teach us so many important lessons.

A Difficult Teen

I know I m hard to handle
A difficult Teen
That doesn't mean you will disgrace me
I have my own issues
I combat with those on daily basis
Situation and circumstances made me so.
I never decided to be this way.
What do I do
If people who came to my life made me what I am today...
When I see my mother crying and father distraughted.
That hurts
I never choose drugs...
How do I tell my sister whatever she is explaining to me.
I have lost my ability to realize or recognize
My urge for this is wild, disobedient and unstoppable.
My body is continuously command for that.
At the end,
Either my heart will bury what it feels
Or my family will bury ME...

When 'Making Love' Turns To 'Sex'

You experience lust not love."
Memories flashed of making love.
Memories flashed of their soul being one.
But those memories lashed her brain.
The more she tries to refrain,
More she ends up in pain.
Chain of memories flooding,
Memories when he made love.
Now that she experience sex with him,
Its tough for her to see their relation spark go dim.
She remembers when they cuddled,
Mind, soul and heart now all muddled.
She had approached him before to get the picture clear.
He felt the fear;
Fear of loosing command on her.
Now she shed pearls from those big beautiful eyes,
She thinks, relationship a short time ago was nice.
But now she begins to realize that love is replaced with lust.
And that's the reason of cracking trust.
She thinks and overthinks the whole night sitting in the balcony,
Now Sun turning the day sunny.
She now turns back to room and laid her swollen eyes on her sleeping mate.
Then grabs a mug of black coffee
And leaves everything on the back of her fate...

Anushka Kesarwani

Anushka Kesarwani is from prayagraj. She has just started writing poems and writes very nicely

.

ज़िन्दगी एक एहसास है जब तक मां बाप का साथ है स्वर्ग और नरक यही है दोस्तों बस ये समझने वाली बात हैं हर कदम पर तुमको जिसने चलना सिखाया ज़िन्दगी से हार ना जाना ये तुम्हे बताया जब रोते थें तो चुप कराया यही है जो अपने दिल के पास है।

ज़िंदगी"

ज़िंदगी बस इक हवा का झोका है कब आता है कब जाता है पता भी नहीं चलता बस यूंही गुजर जाता है इक हल्का सा एहसास छोड़ जाता है ।

ज़िंदगी के हर मोड़ पर कोई मिलता है कोई बिछड़ता है।मिलने में और बिछड़ने में ज़िन्दगी गुजर जाती है। मिलना और बिछड़ना शरीर का है क्यूंकि दिल तो अक्सर जुड़ जाते है और इक एहसास छोड़ जाते हैं।

ज़िंदगी इक कोरा कागज है उसमें मन्न चाहे रंग भर लो कुछ रंग मिटा दो मिट जाते हैं पर कुछ रंग गहरे उतर जाते हैं और इक एहसास छोड़ जाते हैं।

ज़िन्दगी जैसे इक खाली पन्ना हो,स्याही से एक कहानी लिख डालो उस कहानी के पात्र बन कर जिओ कहानी आखिर खतम हो जाती हैं , पर कोई किरदार खूब निभाता है और इक एहसास छोड़ जाता हैं।

ज़िंदगी बहते नदी का पानी है उसमें डुबकी लगा कर देखो वही पानी फिर से छूना नहीं होता बहती रहती धारा इसीकि पानी नहीं ठहरता , ठहरना तो हमको है इसका एहसास छोड़ जाती हैं।

ज़िंदगी के अनगिनत पल में कुछ मीठे कुछ कड़वे पल अतें हैं।हर पल गुज़र जाते है खुश रहना या दुखी ये हमपर लनभयर रहता है लेकिन पल- पल कि इस धड़कन भी इक एहसास छोड़ जाती हैं।

ज़िंदगी जो भी है जैसी भी है इसे समझना बहुत मुश्किल है।ना जान सकते हैं हम ना सुलझा सकते हैं हम इसी उलझी इक सुन्दर सी पहेली हैं लेकिन ज़िन्दगी के इस रंगीन उलझन में कोई आकर कुछ कर- कर दिल छूकर इक एहसास छोड़ जाता हैं।

Deepti Sharma

Deepti Sharma is an engineer, a full-time quants trainer for GMAT & GRE and a freelance author. She loves to write poetry, short-story, plays and stories. Her favourite author is Khaled Hosseini.

Struggling Within

""What happened to my little brother!"" Simran was in a mood to tease her little brother.
""Stop it didi. I am really angry with mom and dad.""
""Why?""
""Coz they produced me on 8th august! I MEAN WHY???""
She laughed. ""Arre! But what's the problem with it?""
""My best-friend Sudhanshu told me that people born on 8th are unlucky and they face troubles throughout their lives.""
""And you think you will face troubles all your life?"" She said pulling his cheek.
He threw her hand away. ""will face troubles means what? I am already facing them!""
""Like?"" She giggled.
""I don't have friends.""
""Aww, such a liar. What about sudhanshu the best friend?""
""No, not at school. At home! I don't have my gully-gang.""

His sister smiled and told him. ""That's nothing kiddo! Real tension is in my life. I have my cricket finals next month after which i will have my twelth boards. Then mom wants me to learn cooking because ""I am a girl"". I also have to write my JEE and NEET coz cricket is just a sport for girls and engineering and medical are the only options available! My hair-fall has doubled. I want to change my glasses and this bloody acne has ruined my face!!!!"" She didn't realize she made the entire house hear it.

Her elder brother, who was cleaning ladyfinger smiled at his mother who was sitting next to him cutting them for the lunch next day. ""what a drama queen your princess is! What does she know about tensions? Tensions are in my life. Those bloody managers have stopped my appraisal and after that fight with my boss the atmosphere of the office is so negative that I hate every second there. And then you guys are over my head dancing 'get married, get married'. I am just 25 but you guys think that's the end of my youth and my life. just get married. whether you love a person or not just get married to her. Irrespective of compatibility, nature and bonding, just find a girl and get married!"" He said with his frustration clear in his voice.

His mother aimed the knife at him. ""have you ever seen yourself in mirror? Which girl will fall for you? Be thankful to God that arranged marriages are still a thing in India. Getting married has become a struggle for today's kids, drama queen. This is not struggle. Struggle is arranging money for your weddings. For simran's college fees. For Pranav's coaching and swimming and god knows how many classes in his school. and then there are a thousand formalities we need to do for society, our in-laws, husband and kids but nobody value our struggles! ""

Her husband who was watching news on tv cut her in. ""Don't be so hard on your son Savitri. Coz you never know what might hurt them and they hang themselves causing troubles for the rest of our life. After my office, I spend my spare time planning about the retirement, the health insurance policies, the FDs, the medical bills, the loans and my son who just goes to a call-centre, sits on his chair, takes 20 tea breaks, enjoys in gym, comes home, enjoys home cooked food, doesn't have to worry about anything and talks about tensions in life. Don't say anything to him Savitri."" He smirked.

The guy threw the cloth he was using to clean the ladyfinger, whispered in his mom's ear. "" Send him to the gym one day, he will know how much i enjoy there."" His mother stared back at him and he started cleaning them again.

The grandfather who was sitting in a corner was trying to soften his chapati by breaking it into pieces and mixing with the milk, looked at his son and the elder grandson. ""Look at you all foolish people talking about problems. At least you don't have to think twice before going to pee. You don't need a stick to walk. You don't have to take medicines more than the food. You don't have to struggle to see or to listen. You don't wake up everyday with the feeling of losing everything! What you talk about is life, not the problems. Foolish people!""
He tried to be louder than the tv and noise of the kids only he couldn't. His voice didn't even surface in the air. And he got busy with his chapati and milk again.

Just above his wheelchair, there was a picture by the wall. Of his late wife, who was observing everyone in the house. There was a sad smile on her lips. At least you all are with each-other."

दा़यरे

कुत्ता कुत्ते को
झूठ झूठ को
खून खून को
नफरत नफरत को
हसरत हसरत को
हिकारत हिकारत को
प्यार प्यार को!

मात खाने वाले इंसान कहलाते है
.....बाकि तो सब एक-दूसरे को पहचान जाते है!

यूँ भी नहीं कि ज़रा नही पहचानते
चोर चोर को
कमज़ोर कमज़ोर को
कामचोर कामचोर को
नौकर नौकर को
पहचान ही जाते हैं।

फिर ये दा़यरे दरम्यान कहाँ से आते है?"

Jatin Senapati

Jatin is from Odisha. Not a regular but writing is his hobby. Insta id-- @heart.scape

My Perplexing Days

I was so perplexed recently,
As if I was missing something very badly,
Like something I left while revelling life,
And now it feels like my heart is being throbbed with knife?
But swiftly I concluded a thing today,
Not missed but something is added to my days,
I am exaggerating feelings all the time,
Which is glemaing matt in my shine"

Anuradha Chakrawarti

Anuradha Chakrawarti ,she's a final year medical student.she belongs to majholi- Jabalpur, Madhya Pradesh.she passionate about her career.she love reading hindi litrature and stories books . Writting is her passion not profession . she's very kind in nature .she believes in sharing love and happiness in the society.

मदद

यह उस समय की बात है जब में नवमी क्लास में पढ़ती थी। में बहुत चंचल स्वभाव की थी,दोस्तो संग मस्ती करना,और बहुत ही मजाकिया मिजाज , यहां तक की में अपने ही टीचर से मजाक कर लेती थी।

और में बहुत सवाली थी हर चीज जानना रहता था मुझे । मेरे घर के पास एक अ◌ा◌ंकल रहते थे, वोह चल नही सकते थे , उनके दो बेटे थे और दोनों उन्हें छोड़ गए ,एक भगवान के पास, दूसरा किसी दूसरे

शहर । एक दिन में स्कूल से आ रही थी और बहुत तेज बारिश होने

लगी ,मेरी सारी दोस्त एक दुकान पर छुप गई और मैं, बारिश बहुत पसंद थी मुझे ,तो में बारिश का मज़ा लेने लगी । पर ये क्या ..?

अचानक मेरी नजर उन अंकल पर पड़ी बारिश की वजह से उनकी

व्हील चेयर गड्ढे में फस गई और वोह उसे निकालने की नाकाम कोशिश करते नजर आए । मैं उनके पास गई और उनकी मदद

करने लगी ,मेरे छोटे हांथो में उतनी ताकत तो ना थी पर मैंने तो

सोच लिया था उनकी मदद करके रहूंगी . मैंने अपनी दोस्त को

आवाज़ दी पर बारिश में भीग जाने के डर से वोह नहीं आई, मैंने भी
उन्हें जाने दिया ,अपना बैग सांभाला और लग है पूरी ताकत से
व्हील चेयर को धक्का देने अंकल भी अपनी पूरी कोशिश करते रहे , आखिरकार
हमारी इरादे सफल हुए और व्हील चेयर गड्ढे से बाहर , मैं बहुत
खुश हुई और अंकल से लगी बोलने देखा अंकल कर लिया ना हमने। पर
अंकल की आांखो से बहते हुए आंसू ने मुझे अन्दर तक झकझोर
दिया ।उन्होंने अपने आंसू पोछ मुझे आशीर्वाद दिया और कहा ,बेटा तुम हमेशा
खुश रहो तुम्हारे सारे सपने पूरे हों ,और वोह चले गए ।
उनके आंसू में मैंने दर्द देखा , अपने अपाहिज होने की लाचारी के साथ उनकी
बेबसी देखी, उस समय इतनी समझ तो ना थी, पर ये समझ गई वोह कितने दुखी थे ।
सोचती हूं अपाहिज वोह थे या हम हैं जो इतने लोगो ने उन्हें देखा
पर किसी ने मदद ना की ,हमारी एक छोटी सी मदद किसी के लिए इतनी बड़ी हो सकती है ।उस दिन मैंने दो चीजें सीखी दोस्ती

का मतलब और मदद की खुशी , किसी की मदद करने में हमारा कुछ नहीं जाता पर जो मिलता है वोह बहुत अनमोल होता है ।

Naveen Shukla

Naveen shukla is from lakhimpur kheri , he is student by profession . He started writing in 2017 . He loves to write and read poetry.

नाराज -: एक शेर ,

मैं जो रूठा तो मनाने नहीं आओगे तुम ,
इक इसी बात से रूठा हुआ हूँ मैं तुमसे

" "एक गजल -:

उसके मुँह से निकल गयी होगी,
बात उसने जब दिल की कही होगी .

,
कह रही थी साथ निभायेगी उम्र भर ,
शायद उसकी जुबान फिसल गयी होगी
.

,
उसको बहुत उम्मीदें थीं महबूब से ,
उसकी मोहब्बत नई नई होगी .

,
ज्यादा दूर नहीं आयी वो मेरे साथ ,
किसी बेहतर को देख के रुक गयी होगी
.

,
तुम्हारे जख्म बहुत हल्के हैं ,
तुमसे शायरी बिल्कुल नहीं होगी .

,
वहाँ सब सच सच बोल रहे थे ,
वहाँ जरूर शराब पी गयी होगी
.

,
अब अंजाम मिला आशिकी में तो जाना ,
""जौन"" तुम्हारी रूह बहुत तड़पी होगी.

Sarita Gawde

"Sarita Gawde,Born and bought up in Hazaribag (Jharkhand). Currently living in the ""city of dreams"" Mumbai.she is a teacher & teaching in JES English medium school in mumbai. She love to listen music.she love to cook & she is a foodie too.she is interested in reading, writing and experimenting new things. She like to tell stories to her students. Her aim in life is to educate students and make them better citizen of India. You can reached to her on insta@saritagawade22

क्रोध का परिणाम

जिंदगी में हर मोड़ पे हमें कुछ न कुछ सीखने को मिलता है। उम्र के हर मोड़ पर कुछ ऐसे अनुभव मिलते जो हमे जिंदगी जीना सीखाते है।जिंदगी का हर अनुभव अलग होता है, हमें उससे कुछ न कुछ सीखने को मिलता है। ऐसा ही एक अनुभव मै आपके साथ साझा करने जा रही हूँ।

मैं अपने परिवार के साथ एक छोटे से शहर में रहती थी। मेरे पिताजी एक स्कूल में शिक्षक थे ।मैं दसवीं कक्षा में थी। मेरे परिवार में कुल मिलाकर पाँच लोग थे। पिताजी, माँ , बड़ा भाई और हम दो बहनें। हमारे पड़ोस में एक बंगाली परिवार रहता था।

उनके एक छोटा बच्चा था । पति-पत्नी के बीच प्यार तो बहुत था पर राजू अंकल के शराब पीकर झगड़ा करने की आदत से गौरी अंटी बहुत दुखी और परेशान रहती थी । अंकल हर रोज शराब पीकर आते और फिर हर छोटी बात पर अंटी से झगडा करते थे ।हर दिन पति-पत्नी के बीच झगड़े होते थे। इस झगड़े से अंटी बहुत परेशान रहती थी।

जब भी झगड़ा होता था। तब अंटी एक बात कहती-" अगर तुमने ये सब बंद नहीं किया तो, मैं एक दिन तुम्हे छोड़ कर चली जाऊँगी ।" एक दिन रोज की तरह अंकल देर रात शराब पीकर आए और फिर से दोनों के बीच झगड़ा हुआ। अंटी ने अंकल को जोर से धक्का दिया, अंकल का सिर दरवाजे से टकराया और वो बेहोश हो गए। अंटी के सब्र का बांध टूट चुका था । अंटी गुस्से में घर से निकल पड़ी। सुबह के कुछ चार बजे होंगे, बच्चे के रोने की आवाज से अंकल को होश आया,उन्होंने देखा की दरवाजा खुला हुआ है। इधर-उधर नज़र दौडाई तो उन्हें अंटी कही दिखाई नहीं दी , वे घबराहट में बाहर गए पर बाहर भी कोई नजर नहीं आया। अब तो उनकी घबराहट बढ़ गई । वे पिताजी के पास आए और सारी बात बताई । पिताजी ने

आस-पड़ोस के कुछ लोगों को इकट्ठा किया और अंटी को ढूंढने निकल पड़े। रास्ते में इधर-उधर देखा पर अंटी कही दिखाई नहीं दी।थोड़ा आगे बढ़ने पर झाडियों में से कुछ आवाज आयी,पिताजी ने टार्च मारकर देखा तो उन्हें एक बड़ा- सा अजगर दिखाई दिया जो पेड़ पर चढ़ रहा था। जब पिताजी ने ध्यान दिया तो समझ में आया कि अभी -अभी अजगर कोई जीव निगला है और उसे हज़म करने के लिए पेड़ पर खुद को लपेट रहा है । अभी पिताजी कुछ सोच भी न पाए थे कि किसी ने कहा –"अरे ये किसकी चप्पल है?" अंकल ने देखा और कहा ये तो गौरी की चप्पल है ।" फिर सारी बातें पिताजी को समझ में आ गई। फिर पिताजी और सब ने मिलकर अजगर को मार डाला । फिर अजगर का पेट चीर कर देखा तो पिताजी का अनुमान सही निकला, गौरी अंटी अजगर के पेट के अंदर थी और हवा न मिलने की वजह से बेहोश हो गई थी । अजगर के पेट के अंदर से गौरी अंटी को बाहर निकाल कर उन पर पानी छिड़का गया। थोड़ी देर बाद उन्हे होश आया तो, उन्हे यकीन नहीं हुआ की वो अभी भी जिंदा है। राजू अंकल को देखते ही वो जोर-जोर से रोने लगी। उन्हें अपने किए पर पछतावा हो रहा था। गौरी अंटी को इस हादसे से एक सीख मिली कि गुस्से में लिया हुआ फैसले की वजह से से जान पर बन सकती है।

क्रोध वह आग है ,जो पल में सब कुछ खाक कर दे,
संयम से लोगे गर काम जरा, तो बिगड़े काम भी जाएँगे बन।
"

Raksha Gupta

रक्षा गुप्ता गाजियाबाद शहर की रहने वाली हैं। उन्होंने तकनीकी शिक्षा से एम. टेक किया है। तथा इंजीनियरिंग कॉलेज में १४ वर्षों तक प्रोफेसर के पद पर कार्य किया है। हिन्दी में रुचि के कारण वह बचपन से ही साहित्य में रुचि रखती थीं। जीवन के हर पहलू पर रचनाएँ लिखना उनका शौक है।

रचना विषय- रोष

हँसा करती थी वह ऐसे हरदम,
जैसे लहरें गुनगुनाएँ सरगम...
छोटी छोटी खुशियों में भी,
हृदय किया करता था स्पन्दन..

मेहनत से कभी न घबराती वह,
हर काम झपट ही निपटाती वह..
देख न पाती किसी का क्रन्दन,
हँसा करती थी वह ऐसे हरदम...

असुर प्रकृति का आया एक दानव,
मन मस्तिष्क से पूर्णतः अमानव..
छीन ली खुशियाँ,बांट दिये गम,
हँसा करती थी वह ऐसे हरदम....

आज भी हृदय में रोष है इतना,
प्रचण्ड रूप ज्वाला के जितना..
सबक सिखाने का भरती है दम,
हँसा करती थी वह ऐसे हरदम

नीयत

क्यों देते हो तुम दोष प्रभु को,
खुद की नीयत को देखो तो...
उसके वजूद को आंकने वालों,
खुद के अस्तित्व को तोलो तो...

क्या है मन में हनुमत सी भक्ति,
या लक्ष्मण जैसा त्याग बसा...
किस हक से चाहो श्रीराम का संग,
जब हृदय में रावण सा अहम् भरा..

मन में चाहिए छवि राम की,
नजरें और भाव अमर्यादित हैं..
शबरी सी प्रतीक्षा करना न जानो,
मन प्रति पल तेरा उन्मादित है...

ईश्वर की अद्‌भुत रचना का,
अपमान तुम पल पल करते हो ..
दोषारोपण की आदत तुमको,
स्वयं ध्वंस सृजन को करते हो..

मौलिक एवं स्वरचित
रक्षा गुप्ता

जज्बात

संवादों की इस दुनियाँ में,
जज्बातों को आराम नहीं..
कहना चाहूँ अब और मैं क्या,
कहने को बची कोई बात नहीं..

मन मस्तिष्क विचारों का दंगल,
उलझन प्रति पल आबाद हुई..
हर क्षण उनको सुलझाने में,
अगणित जिज्ञासा बरबाद हुई..

कहना चाहूँ अब और मैं क्या,
कहने को बची कोई बात नहीं..

उत्साह भरा जब नव ऊर्जा का,
दायित्व की चपला संचार हुई...
भावुकता के पसरे आंचल में,
अश्रुओं की बौछारें कई बार हुई...

कहना चाहूँ अब और मैं क्या,
कहने को बची कोई बात नहीं..

स्वार्थी रिश्ते

नहीं दिया कभी समय स्वयं को,
गलत सदा यह अपने साथ किया
सबकी खुशियों को कर्तव्य मान,
जी-जान से उसका निर्वाह किया..

घटिया नीयत का अनुमान न था,
हर कदम पर हमने साथ दिया..
जब पड़ी जरूरत मुझको अब,
स्वार्थियों ने गैरों का नाम दिया..

झूठे रिश्तों की सच्चाई दिखाने को
शायद कुदरत ने एक खेल रचा..
भावुक हृदय तो मेरा सम्भल गया
पर सन्देश मुझे अनमोल मिला..

कल उगने वाला अटल दिवाकर,
नव स्वर्णिम सुबह ही लायेगा..
जिसमें होंगे केवल वे ही रिश्ते,
जिन्हें अंतर्मन सत्य बताएगा...

मौलिक एवं स्वरचित

Feroz Ahmad Dar

He is FEROZ AHMAD DAR.He is from Kashmir. He is a research scholar. He loves to write poetry.He is amicable and benevolent. (12)

(Beyond Barricades And Boundaries Of Covid 19)

Feroz Ahmad Dar
Talangam Pulwama

There has been a complete lockdown by government on the wrath of Covid 19 across the country. People are also restrained from buying the necessary items and only a selected portion of time has been ratified for buying and selling of essential commodities. Although it is very important for all of us to follow the guidelines because this virulent disease is effecting us at a very fast pace and badly. We should track the precautions issued by the Ministry of Health. However, an important aspect of this Covid 19 has been free time. Now the question props up, how do we make use of this free time?, How do we consume and utilize it in a proper manner without getting used to something as bad as PUBG these days. We know because of this pandemic people have been seized to their respective homes. The same fraternity of people gets bored, therefore, many switched over to social media, Tv, online games etc. People have become homesick. They are busy with online games and other falsehood activities. One can easily asses the regard we have failed to give to time. Let's not forget the very commonly used expression with regard to the utility of time "Time and Tide waits for None" .So let's wake up before it's too late. There are quite a few quarries that struck our mind while we contemplate over this thought doing away with waste of Time. Some of the quarries are:

How do we forget the vices that we are attached to nowadays? We know it that "Allah is happy with those who don't have intention to waste time". Let's see how can we engage ourselves with time without wasting it or what are the things so that Allah will be happy with us. let's know....(1)primarily we must organize a strategy for present to offer prayers five times a day jointly in our homes. (2)These lockdown holidays would be the golden period for our progeny if we lecture them about the history of our religion, the seerat of our prophet Mohammad (PUBH)the excitement of our sahaba besides their necessary education.(3)Further, our brood can be trained in learning Quran and Hadees. For a little bit we can wear and tear on networking sites to envisage constructive and effective videos. (4)During this complete lockdown there were many families who have been without provisions and other eatables for large number of days. We must develop a system so that the timely help reaches to such families as innumerable voluntarily organizations are helping these families, why not do our bit too to satisfy our human consciousness. Ensure we are doing it to please Allah, not to take selfi and embarrass these needy people. Not to see yourselves on the newspaper headlines but only for a genuine and noble cause.

The single motive behind discussing these eventful things is to ensure that we manage time properly learn to use it efficiently ,build an atmosphere where the essence of time is made clear to our children irrespective of whatever age he or she may be. We should engage ourselves in healthy discussion debates, or good deeds. We must Thank Allah for HIS bounties and no doubt Time is one of them. "

Blind Justice

How ruthless life is without a breath
Killings had been named an ultimate death
All gone want justice and it remaining dream
Oh!How ruthless life is,how can a dumb scream.
What our water bodies want to say?
Innocents are being dumped into their way
But,no never we can understand
If nature want to hold justice in our hand
Innocents are suppressed by imperealisti wands
How long the blood run through our lands
There is no one for the people to believe
All are selfish all to deceive
Oh! God shower your blessings on us
Destroy those who wants war and creates fuss."

My Mother)

She is like a flower that blooms at the day
She is very sweet and great for me everyday
She is a precious gift from God
Who always listens to me with a nod
Her thinking is very high
Which tends to fly
She always takes my Care
Because I always fear
She always teaches me to give
Without her I will never live."

Piyush Kumar

He is Piyush Kumar who lives in Ranchi . He's perusing PGDM from Ranchi , he loves writing poetry and also interested in singing .

एक चुप्पी

ज़िन्दगी में एक वक़्त पर चुप रहना भी
कभी ना कभी काम आ जाता है

ये थोड़ी सी चूपी , और कुछ पल का समय
कभी ना कभी सामने बाले को चुप करा जाता है

सोचना छोड़ दो अब ये , की ज़िन्दगी कहां तक जाएगी
कहीं भी जाएगी कुछ अच्छा ही कर दिखाएगी

बस खुद पर भरोसा और अपने हौसला को बुलंद रख
फिर देखना उस मंजर को , जब वो मंजर इतिहास में रची
जाएगी।।।।।।।" " ज़िन्दगी की करीबी

हमनें अक्सर ज़िंदगी को क़रीब से देखा है
कुछ दूर हुए लम्हों को क़रीब से देखा है

आंखो के सामने छाई अंधेरों से पूछा जब मैंने,
तो उस तरफ़ से आयी आवाज को महसूस कर देखा है

दूर तक चलकर किनारों की तलाश करता रह गया ,
हमने बेबस और लाचार परिंदो को भी संभलते देखा है

कहीं ज़िन्दगी के भाग दौड़ में अपने ना छूट जाए
इस बातो को हक़ीक़त में दिल से लगाकर देखा है

हां ,,,हमने अक्सर ज़िंदगी को क़रीब से देखा है
कुछ दूर हुए लम्हों को क़रीब से देखा है

मैंने ज़िन्दगी से सीखा है ।

मैंने ज़िन्दगी से सीखा है , खुद में खुश रहना ।
मैंने ज़िन्दगी से सीखा है , खुद को मेहसूस करना ।
मैंने ज़िन्दगी से सीखा है , खुद पर यकीन करना ।
मैंने ज़िन्दगी से सीखा है , एक वक़्त पर चुप रहना
मैंने ज़िन्दगी से सीखा है ,
एक दूसरे कि मदद करते रहना ।
मैंने ज़िन्दगी से सीखा है ,
समय की जरूरतों को समझते रहना ।
मैंने ज़िन्दगी से सीखा है ,अच्छे वक़्त को लाने के
लिए हमेशा प्रयास करते रहना ।
मैंने ज़िन्दगी से सीखा है ,
कामयाबी की एक बड़ी सोच में रहना ।

Palak Inwati

Her name is Palak. She is from seoni (m.p). She is study in medical field. Her only dream is to make proud and publishe her own book. She loves ,traveling, reading write up. She spread positivity all around..

जिंदगी को समझना

चाहते तो है हम इस ज़िन्दगी को समझना
पर जितना समजने की कोशिस करो ,
उतना ही उलझा देती है ये ज़िन्दगी,
इस ज़िन्दगी की कश्मकस को जो समजता है,
वही इस ज़िन्दगी जी पाता है।

ज़िन्दगी हमे इसे इंसानों से मिलवाती है,
जिन्हें हम जान से ज्यादा प्यार करते है,
फिर ये ज़िन्दगी इसे मोड़ पे खड़ा करती है,
जिसको हम जान से ज्यादा चाहते है,
वाही बिच राह में छोड़कर चला जाता है,

ज़िन्दगी को क्या मिलता है ये सब करके,
दिल तो हमारा तडपता है दुरिया सहके,
ज़िन्दगी अपना काम करके जाती है,
हम कितना भी खुश रह ले,
एक दिन ये हमे रुलाती है,

ज़िन्दगी क्यों हमे मिली है ,
जीने के लिए या मरने के लिए मिली है।

क्यों इसे हम समज नहीं पाते ,
क्यों खुद की मर्जी से जी नहीं पाते ,
बहुत ऐसे सवाल है,
जिनके जवाब अभी बाकी है ,
और नए सवाल इसमें जुड़ते जाते है

Lalitha Srinivas

"Lalitha Srinivas , born in Andhra Pradesh on 29-11-1994. She has a Bachelor's degree in Computer Science from Jawaharlal Nehru Technological University. She has been part of many anthologies as a co-author. She is a home maker, attune to create a beautiful art, either it's with ink filled in pen on a paper or brush dipped in paint on a canvas. She is a traveller, who wish to explore the beauty of INDIA, rejoice different cultures and different cuisines. She started writing in her page at Instagram and dedicate it to her late friend who committed suicide. She is inspiring people by interacting with them and understanding their pains, who are in verge of committing suicide. Whenever you feel alone, ping her on.

Insta I'd: @celebrate_golden_days.

Or

Mail: @srijaan4111@gmail.com

Self Esteem

I am walking away,
from those LOVE
crowned with thrones.
Wearing it is too painful.
Without that crown,
May I can't be said to be your queen.
But it's better to be stay
As a princess without you.

Judgemental

Now -A-Days Judging Others
Become A Beautiful Art..
X :""Do You Know?? He Have A Gf""..
Y: ""Oh!! Ya, But She Won't Worth Him""..
X: ""Do You Know?? She Broke Up""..
Y: ""Omg!! She Is A Gold Digger"". I Know!
But GUYS!!!
Beautiful CREATION Of Your ART
Is An Ugly DESTRUCTION Of
Someone's HEART."   "

Trust.

If Someone Don't Trust You Once.
Belief On You Will Never Regain.
Eventhough They Say
""I TRUST YOU"".
It Will Be Waste Of Time
By Convincing Them For Lifetime..

Pain

When I look at the past,
I see pain overcome the happiness..
Memories of past..
Either good or bad..
Hurts alot..
Because they didn't last forever..

Admire

Admiring Someone Is Not A Big Deal.
But!! Letting That Someone,
Admire You Is A Big Deal..
Deal With Yourself.
To Be An Inspiring Person."   "

Time.

Time Is Moving Like A ROCKET.
It Changed Everything.
But Still My Heart Struck.
On That Time Period.
When I First Fall In LOVE.
Even I'm Living In This Modern World.
My HEART Still Living With
Memories Of Those Golden Days.

Dream.

I was in a deep sleep.
Dreaming about our future.
Memorizing our moments.
Planning our wedding.
But when I woke up.
You was not there with me.
Feeling it as a nightmare.
I'm unable to sleep anymore.

Shreya Vij

She is a young writer,17
Her poetries are penned when her emotion find thoughts and thoughts found its word!!
She is optimistic and motivated to gain best out of life..
All her writings were posted in @poetic_.soull"

A Newspaper Headline

It was a rainy dayy..
I was on bed and radio played.
Got my eyes on table where an old newspaper layed...
Saw one of its headline which left me amazed.

The heading announces an arrival of a spaceship todayy...
With that heading i got carried away.
Bought my telescope and sat near the window pane..
Waiting for the spaceship the day paseed away.

Sky got dark stars shine bright..
Suddenly between them i saw a beam of light.
Thinking it was a spaceship i jumped off my place...
Screamed and called everyone at my place.

After a few moments mom started laughing
On asking her she murmered,
It was nt the space ship but a shooting star that you saw.
And the newspaper you read had came few days ago..
Listening to this i got sad and went to hit a sack..
Laughing on myself for such silly act.

Growing Older

Growing older isn't as amazing as it sounds to be,
Weight of books now seems lighter than that of a world,
It was easier to get up early than having the sleepless nights
Doing homework was much better than doing all the work,
class tests seems much easier than the life tests,
Now that eagerness of growing up sounds stupid,
But As there is no comeback so we have to accept this fact!!

Rajan V Kokkuri

Rajan V Kokkuri hailing from Attoor,Kerala, an Engineering Designer by profession is working with Worley in Muscat. Rajan is the author of two books by name 'I Remain Forever Yours' and 'My Precius Dreams'. Rajan has Co-Authored 'Life in Lockdown' and seven other books. Rajan's 2nd book 'My Precius Dreams' was published in August 2020 has been trending in the Amazon Kindle Best Sellers list. Rajan's book 'I Remain Forever Yours' was among 'Top Debut Writer Novels in 2019 selected by Literatureslight. Kokkuri has also won Delslam weekly poem contests also. Rajan is a well known person among Social Cultural circle of Muscat too.

The Flight To Toronto

(Short Story)

My cousin Ravi dropped me by auto at the entrance of Chatrapati International Airport, Bombay. The weather was nice, slight breeze was there. 31 January 1992, Air-India, BBY-DXB' I checked my air ticket while walking towards the check-in counter along with three newly recruited persons. The staff was very friendly and told me. 'Sir, the flight is over booked and we are giving you business class seat.' Hearing the type of seat my co-passenger smiled at me. We reached Dubai and was picked by a Philipino driver to take us to Abhudhabi. The first drive itself had given me excitement due to the wide roads and the high speed of the car. I was the only Cad Designer selected by the company from a group of twenty five people. I joined the company and collegues were from Philippines. I had lot of unforgettable incidents to remember. My boss by name was Howard Russell. Once during lunch time he became very disturbed and called me. 'Raj, my lunch got stuck in the table drawer.' I replied, 'Yes, Sir'. Howard continued 'Call Ali Sudani, and ask him to break the lock' Soon Ali reached and opened the drawer. Howard felt very happy and thanked Ali. I was very keen to find out what was boss lunch packet. He took out an apple and started eating. I looked at Ali and winked my eyes. Howard ate apple for lunch but was very lavish to order pizza once in a week and he always made a point to invite our department members. Howard had a official Toyota Camry car and he used to take me often to our client office. Once there was big bomb blast and threat was there for many expatriates. My colleagues warned me travelling with my boss. I stood firm with my boss Howard to visit the client offices. Due to these reasons friendship grew well. He liked me very much and that has helped me to grow in the company as Cad Coordinater soon. We used to have night shift also. One of colleague Leo had a girl friend who lived in USA. Leo received once a call from his girlfriend. We all were bachelors and had a boring life. Leo took the receiver and after speaking he had given the receiver to me and later to my friend Jo. Jo took the phone and was feeling nice to talk. Jo said, 'Leo has nice person to chat, but we are also bachelors and there is no entertainment for us.' Hearing this the USA girlfriend replied 'No problem, I will talk to you people also.' We used to have such nice fun. One of our designer Romy was slow in doing work. We helped in completing his work and return we had lot of nice food and entertainment during the night shift. We had another friend by name Bingo and he was always had the habit of hearing one old radio songs loudly. We got fed up of this sound disturb and I took the transistor and hit on floor while he was away. Next day Bing found out that the radio is not working any more, he went and complained to our Engineering manager. Even though we didn't get any punishment our entertainments were curtailed by the management. Days passed. It was one Friday lunch time. Our lunch was at a Kerala restaurant which was ten minutes walking distance. I and my close friend Kumar was walking back to our company guest house. It was sudden that something strong hit my leg strongly and I sat on the road. Kumar hit a glass piece by leg and I stamped over it. My leg started bleeding heavily. I didn't remember anything much after that and reached the clinic in city by company driver soon. The nurse over there was our colleague Mario's wife and timely care helped me to recover soon. The rent was very high during those days. Soon my family arrived in Abhudhabi and our bachelor days was over. I and my friend Subin took a flat together. There are few interesting episodes happened during family days. It was very difficult to get family visa during those days. My wife Ana and son arrived. Days passed. Once my friend and I was going to office and his car hit someone. Police took him to police station. I hurried back to our flat and informed his wife. I had told to pack lunch for him The rules were very and I thought he may not get good in police staton.Luckily he was released soon and we headed to office. Another funny thing happened during few days later. We were ready to leave and went downstairs. We noticed that the car was missing from the parked place. We got panic and didn't know how to handle the situation and started our walk towards the police station. The police informed us it is usual over there so do not worry. On the way back we found the car was parked in the side of road few metered way from our home. This incidents continued and we kept ourself sleepless and tried to find out the thief. We didn't succeeded in finding the thief but Subin purchased a new car later. Our family friendship circle grew and the closest family friend was by name Bala. He owned a car before me and helped us for our trips. Once we were coming on the highway and his car tyre became puncture. We were escaped from major accident with the help of a national we reached home safely. He had a daughter by name Poorni. She was very friendly with my son Rahul. Bala and family migrated to Canada and we stayed back.

In the company my job became very tedious. I had the responsibility of managing a group of people who were doing night duty. On that particular day I was driving to office at around 4am and crossed at the last minute of signal when it was turning to red. I was thinking it was ok, but saw police chasing me from back and blinked the light. I had parked the car and reached the officer. He spoke in Arabic 'kalaboose (hand clutches). I understood that since he showed action by hand. I had started shivering. There were two officers. I had pleaded and one officer felt sorry for me and left after giving punishment ticket. I reached office and had another surprise was waiting for me. The designer didn't complete the work assigned to him. Soon the piping engineer came to me to know the status of work. He found that work was not over he hit me on the right shoulder. I felt huge pain and sat down covering my face. I didn't complaint to the management considering they might terminate both of us. The tough period was over soon and better time arrived for me. I was made Cad Coordinater and received benefits too. I got opportunity to get trained with various training and also attended overseas seminar with the engineering manager. There was no reason to look back and moved to Oil and Gas leading companies in Doha and Muscat.

There was an announcement. 'We are going to reach Toronto soon'. I took out the wedding invitation from my bag and showed to my co passenger. 'Sir, do you know this address in Toronto.' He looked at my face with surprise and replied. 'Oh, this is close to my place, I will drop you., it is near Sree Krishna temple around half an hour drive from the airport. ' I replied 'Thank you sir, I want give surprise to my friend Bala who was with me in Abhudhabi.' He said, 'My name is Colin.' He continued. 'What brings you to Canada?' I was very happy and replied. 'My friend' Bala's daughter Poorni is getting married tomorrow. I will be seeing them after twenty years. We were very close when he was in UAE'. Colin smiled and took my hand and shook. 'I adore your great friendship.' The announcement was in the air. To-day is 20th August and local time in Toronto is 8am.We are landing soon in Toronto International Airport, outside temperature is 20 degree celcious' Thank you for flying KLM. I got ready to get down. The End." Nil Nil

Kavita Misra

"Instinctively socially conscious, romantic by approach, well connected to modern trends, in thinking and lifestyle, Kavita is viewing the world through the prism of detached observation, absorbing and fulminating on the different shades of the spectrum that symbolize modern, work-a-day life, where monotony rules but not contentment and satisfaction.

She had her schooling from St Fidelis College and Christ Church College, graduated from I.T. College and did her B.Ed from Navyug Degree College. She has taught in CMS and Red Hill School, and is now a freelance translator and blogger, equally adept and fluent in English and Hindi.

You can find her on-

Instagram as @literarykavita and on Facebook as Literary kavita. She writes blogs at @kavita- thinking aloud"

The Experience Called 'Marriage'

Are you there? No. Few days back someone told me that you breathed your last. Since the day I met you for the first time, I knew that you will be an important part of my life, forever. "Important", you remained till the end and you are even today, but "part of life"? Well, I'm not quite sure of that.

You have always been there in my personal diary...as my 'fantasy' before I met you, as my 'would be husband'
when I met you, as my 'life' when we stayed together and as my past ever since I came back from your house to my parental home.

And what I wished to say to you was never the same as was expected from me. When we first met, people expected me to say "I respect you", but we had got so close that I could easily say "I love you". When we were together, I saw the real YOU. Then, what I said was "I love you" but I told only my personal diary how much I hated you.

What was evident, was that I had carried bags full of my belongings when I went to you, and came back empty-handed. But my diary will tell you the truth... that I had come to you with nothing from my past, but came back with a bag full of feelings, emotions, memories all wrapped up in abuses, both verbal and physical.

As the years passed, people could see the bag as it was now bulging with all the rough stuff, so much so that things sprang out of it every now and then. Seeing my baggage, people were sure now that I hated u. But my diary read "I pity you" because the best part of our marriage - our daughter, came with me.

Now, when you are gone, just before the last tie between us was about to break, history repeats itself. What people expect me to say is ... that I feel nothing for you, my diary whispers "I miss you".

Atul yadav

Atul belongs to Rohtak district in Haryana.He loves to write poems.He writes for his inner peace. Soon, he is going to join Indian Army.

INSTAGRAM- immature__guy

तुम, चाय और इश्क़

इतनी जल्दी कहां चले??
फिर से दोहराने कुछ किस्से रंगीन बाकी हैं...
तमन्नाएं गिनवाना तुम अपनी
तुम्हारी हर बात पर कहना आमीन बाकी है...
दो कप चाय और मंगा ले??
रुक जाओ ना , अभी तो शाम हसीन बाकी है।

धर्म हूं मै

धर्म हूं मैं, मुझे बांटा लोगो ने बहुत हिस्सों में
पर किसी हिस्से में भी इंसानियत की महक नहीं..
कहने को सब मेरी मर्जी से होता है
फिर मन मुताबिक़ मोड़ लिया गया मुझे,
इसमें भी कोई शक नहीं,
मेरे नाम पे इंसानियत की हत्या करते आए हैं
मुझे जीने का कोई हक नहीं....

निरा इश्क़ है तु

जिस्मानी इश्क़ के दौर में, तेरा नज़रे मिलना
तुमने तो जायज के पैमाने बदल दिए...
मुझे सोते देख तेरा नजर का टीका लगाना,
हाये! तुमने तो इश्क़ के मायने बदल दिए..

मृगतृष्णा

तेरी यादों के अंगारों में पल पल ये बदन जलता है,
तेरे पास होने का एहसास तो लगता महज़ मृगतृष्णा है...
ठहरा है सब कुछ वहीं, ना वक़्त ज़रा भी चलता है,
न खुर्शीद खिला है कब से, न ही ढलती ये रात कृष्णा है...

Anzar Usmani

Anzar belongs to city of tehzeeb,Lucknow.His origin itself defines his keen interest and passion towards poetry.He has a thunder of words trembling within him.The day he feel low or he feel down,will be the day when he will pen down another master combination of words in a poetry.His belief is that if a poet is having some grief or pain in his/her heart,then he/she will give the best poetry of themselves that day.

Thoughtful Night

Last night i was staring at that stars,
Thinking how to skip out that bars.
No ,staring is not what i desire,
No,thinking is not what i require.

All my thoughts were poping in my brain,
It was no less than a heavy rain.
""Its nothing more than overthinking""one of those star said.
You will be realizing it when all leaves of your hope shed.

Tired of all my thoughts i tried to sleep
Stopped me one of those thoughts that ""am i so weak""
Just like frost freezes the water on window pane,
These thoughts ceases the worker in my brain.

A knock in my head say,till the end which will stay-
""Stop counting on stars,life is like dark night
Else you would be taken far by one of those large tides""

My own thinking seemed to be the reason of my fall,
My eyes welled up when all the loses i recall.

I hope all these evil thoughts will be gone,
By the striking of sunray of the dawn
Else i would have to make my brain frown
Then hopes of positive thoughts would be sown.

The Regrets

Yes, i am a sinner,
Just consider me as fake.
I am just a ditcher,
It was not your mistake.

I proved my promises wrong and all i gave you is tears.
All that happiness for so long,
Has turned into fears.

Ohh girl its your life,
Dont let others rule.
Yeah its your story,
You have to be cruel.

I know its all my mistake,
All the feelings that i bury.
Just a thing left to ask,
Is it too late to be sorry.

मंज़िल

तू आया है इस दुनिया मै,
तू अपनी ज़िंदगी ख़ुद बनाएगा |
जितना ही तू तोड़ेगा ख़ुद को,
उतना मज़बूत बनता जाएगा |

अपनी नज़र रख बस मंज़िल पे,
तुझे कोई डर ना सताएगा |
कोई नहीं रहेगा हाँ साथ तेरे,
तू खुद ही खुद को बचाएगा |

उस दिन भूख मिटेगी तेरी,
जब ख़ुद के लिए एक रोटी कमाएगा |
ख़ुद को कामयाब देखने के लिए,
जब तू पुराने ज़ख़्म भुलाएगा |

टूट के जुड़ने का है सफर ये,
यही तुझे मंज़िल तक पहुंचाएगा |
इस सफर में अपनों से बिछड़ की ही,
तू ख़ुद से मिल पाएगा |"

Monika Goswami

She says she choose her diary to express her thoughts. That is how she communicates with her inner self. She's Monika Goswami, from Uttarakhand. She's a 21 year old college student pursuing Biotechnology from Jaipur. Basically an outgoing person, a full time dreamer and a nature lover. She's a little ball of sunshine emitting the radiant wherever she goes.

Believe

He created the talent within since childhood,
As he was inspired by a great personality.
He learned with consistency.
His growth was at its peak.
He went smoothly and relentlessly.
Couldn't excel well in studies initially,
But the end was marvelous for him.
He's a radiant ball of sunshine now.
That was not an easy task.
Even went hungry at days to achieve his passion.
Now he celebrates every now and then for his achievements.
He said yes to fewer things.
Materials objects were of no interest to him!!
Health was his top priority.
He was kind enough.
Faced heartbreak but didn't stop,
He honored his scars in the best ways.
He's inevitable now.
Oh! Look what storms made out of him.
Pinch of thunder and lightning run through his veins.
An alpha personality was built within!!

Last Salutation

And here's a last salutation to-
The MUFFLED CRIES we made for that unworthy love in our life!!
A last salutation to-
The times when we UNLOVED OURSELVES and,
Considered others opinion a greater priority!!
A last salutation to-
The LIES heard from a fake lover!!
A last salutation to-
The JUDGEMENTS made from the society!!
A last salutation to-
The Times when we ignored our LOVED ONES!!
Let's accept the fact that we all make mistakes and,
It's okay to do so!!
But the foremost thing is acceptance of the mistakes been made.
And one should learn to evolve from them and,
Not let them take over our minds!!
So today let's make self love a bigger priority!!

Freedom

Freedom is a state of mind.
It's not your clothes, your hair,
Or the type of friend circle you hold.
It's not taking drugs,
It's not the love affairs!!
Freedom is how earthly your thoughts are,
Your choices!!
Your decisions reflect how free your mind is.
When you fight for freedom in terms of physical factors,
It's simply a purportedly protest.
Freedom comes when you stop caring of what others think of you!!
Stop searching for it in material objects,
Rather search it within!!

Sayani Bag

A writer by passion and not by profession. Her latest composition is available in the book " It's All About Me and You". She writes and paints her soul on @_poetries.of.blue_

What Is Life?

Life is mystic. Life is unpredictable.
One day so much and one day withered off.
Life is a roller coaster ride in between,
The rise and the fall which defines your journey,
Emotions and people; Priorities and Inferiorities,
Dreams and Reality; Destiny and Fate,
Peace and War, Wounds and Scars,
Pain and Sufferings; Success and failures,
Good and Evil; Facts and Mysteries,
Life is a book of beautiful memories,
Everyone has its own story,
We meet so many people in your life.
With every new person comes a new experience in life,
Some make you feel like you are their top priority, whereas some make you feel unwanted,
Some will break our trust, whereas some will love you
Some will hug you tight, whereas some will let you go easily,
Some will say hello excitedly, whereas some will say goodbye with teary eyes.
Life is a series of experiences, Life is a reason,
The experience of life will mature you and teach you,
It will teach you to be happy, to be sad, to love,
It will teach you the difference between right and wrong,
And most importantly it will teach you even after giving up everything it wasn't worth it,
Childhood will teach you that life is a series of experiences,
But adulthood will make you experience it,
Don't be shocked to find your expectations wrong.
Life doesn't go on the way we expect,
Because we don't get back what we did for someone,

Life will give you happiness, yet you'll have scars from your memories,
Life will give you attachments, yet you'll feel lonely,
But every experience will have some positivity,
The experiences might not always be pleasant, but it will teach you a lesson,
Life is yours, so design it the way you want it to be.

Keerthi Ravishankar

Her metanoia with writing is just the prevail of her messed up life and unsure promises. Slayed by life,she got into writing which healed her scars.Yup ,a 20 yrs old literature nerd she is.""Lost everything but got writing"".She is a heavy hearted soul longing for love attaining it by giving to those who long .More than a writer,she wants to be a socialist.

Her anger towards the society turned into words thru the pen. She usually looks the world in her point of view which is extremely controversial to the realistic parameters.She loves her friends like family and can do anything for them nomatter it is right or not.

Moreover she is an observer and hearer of sensual things. Lately, she named her pen as A BEAUTIFUL BREATHE OF LIFE, AVALYN that she breathes just because of it.

""I wander for specific,missed things in what I was""

To me""writing is how I breathe by"".

IF YOU CAN WRITE,YOU CAN HEAL"

Day And Night

The circle of life
Radiied with the invaluable!!
Liquored with love
Lessoned with life!
The day cries
The night laughs
The day smiles!
The night screws!
Evanescent evils!
Empowering the devils!
Sometimes you're hard!
To be heard!
Sometimes you're longed!
To be lamped!
It's our smile's bark!
Itched to be smashed dark!
But it's our smile's!
Smashes in the bark of the dark!
Cry carries crane of grey!
Cleansed by the smile in day!
Devil deited is a day- show
Devil drowned is a night-show
Day counts The smiles of faces
Night counts sprain of hearts

Life

AW!why you're so arduous to me?
Why you're so leaden?
Ecstatic isn't a state, for me too?
Amn't I'm scrummy?
I know you're a boorish adroit,
But have some lenience!
Are you a whippersnapper?
Not at all obliging,
Such a obfuscate!
Is Insouciant, a nightmare?
Regret! Incoginant I am!
Heartstrings outran,
Cordolium Camped!
Haven't I battered?
Repleted with sensorium?
You're meddling ,Brute!
I beseech,zip it!
I'm hammered,I'm frazzled,
I'm ruptured,I'm maimed.
Don't you chortle at me even?
For lighting you, the entire!"

Sonali Joshi

Sonali Joshi metis/mixed blood writer, originally from Rajsthan, living in the cleanest city of India yes 'Indore' since 1996. She has published her poetry 'Zindagi ka Aaina' in this book & she had been worked as a co-author in many books also. She is writing on today's reality, social issues and motivational aspects too. She is a silver medalist in minor research project at college level and also be the part of Anti-ragging committee in our college. She is a creative & curious person in nature. Singing, dancing, poetry writing, telling, anchoring & influencer are the special hobbies of her. Kindness, truth and honesty are the main mantras of her life. Follow her for creative and motivational Poetry on @sonalijoshi78 on instagram and sonali joshi poetry on you-tube.

जिंदगी का आईना'

मैं मनुष्य हूँ,
हाँ मैं, मनुष्य हूँ!!
अनोखा है, व्यक्तित्व मेरा,
औरो से कुछ अलग है, अस्तित्व मेरा!
कभी कई विषादों से घिरा, तो
कभी कई उम्मीदों से बँधा है, चरित्र मेरा!!
मैं मनुष्य हूँ,
हाँ मैं, मनुष्य हूँ!!
कहने को सकल चलता हूँ,
दौड़ाने को अकल चलता हूँ!
कहने को मैं मुक्त हूँ, पर
कहीं न कहीं, समाज के बंधनों से युक्त हूँ!!
मैं मनुष्य हूँ,
हाँ मैं, मनुष्य हूँ!!
टूटता हूँ, गिरता हूँ, उठता हूँ,
फिर सम्भलकर चलता हूँ!
उम्मीदों के पुँज का, मैं
कहीं न कहीं, पीछा करता हूँ!!
मैं मनुष्य हूँ,
हाँ मैं, मनुष्य हूँ!!
मैं वहम में हूँ,
अपने ही अहम में हूँ!
कभी महफ़िल में अकेला हूँ,
तो कभी अकेले होकर भी, खुद मे मशरूफ हूँ!!
मैं मनुष्य हूँ,
हाँ मैं, मनुष्य हूँ!!

प्रेम अपार हैं, मन में
थोड़ा सा ईर्ष्या का भी व्यवहार हैं मेरा!
आचार तो हैं, एक जैसे मगर
हर तर्क पर, थोड़ा अलग ही हैं विचार मेरा!!
मैं मनुष्य हूँ,
हाँ मैं, मनुष्य हूँ!!
खुद की इच्छाओ को छिपाकर,
अक्सर अपनों के लिए, मनन करता हूँ!
कहता हूँ खुद के लिए भाग रहा हूँ!
किंतु बिन विचारे खुद से अधिक, अपनो के लिए जतन करता हूँ!!
मैं मनुष्य हूँ,
हाँ मैं, मनुष्य हूँ!!
कभी इच्छा तो कभी अनिच्छा से
इस दुनिया की रस्मो को, अदा करता हूँ!
बिन शब्द के अपने चरित्र के दर्पण को सब के समक्ष, अर्पण करता हूँ!!
मैं मनुष्य हूँ,
हाँ मैं, मनुष्य हूँ!!
परिस्तिथिया हो विपरीत, या हो बुरा मंजर
उम्मीद का दामन थामे, अपने पथ पर अग्रसर रहता हूँ!
खुद को सिद्ध करने के लिए,
आजीवन जतन करता हूँ!!
मैं मनुष्य हूँ,
हाँ मैं, मनुष्य हूँ!!"

Gayatri Gor

Gayatri Vinod Gor - a stranger soul for most of this world. She was born on 12th April, 1988 for making her life little creative and beautiful. She has been a bright star at all the levels of her life. With the pure innocence in this unknown world, she has earned a good amount of maturity with the innermost fierce struggle. She always wanted to share her experiences with all the beautiful souls around her. One day she found pen and paper from an untouched mind. She held that pen looking the an infinite sky and started writing her own little world with the help of this universe. She knows that she will bloom beautifully. She will keep writing more and more to unfold the pleasant fragrance all around.

Instagram I'd- lovelygayu534

Stay Strong

1. This undefeated spirit of mine is made up of burns, pains, wounds, tears, scars, screams and sufferings.

2. I used to think that no one can fix me but magical souls and vibes do exist on this Earth.

3. Everything can go to hell in less than a second but you need to do whatever it takes to survive. Survival is life till the ultimate death.

4. I don't want to be in this world. I want to travel through those stars, set my goals and come back.

Spread Love

5. You need to be gentle with your heart because it knows your pain and heals it too.

6. I strongly recommend self love. Stop looking for your worth in people or productivity.

7. Dont expect that someone else will relate to your pain. It's yours, just yours.

Create Your Own World

8. I become wordless when it comes to writing us.

9. Don't dwindle yourself for perfection. Little messy things looks cute sometimes.

10. God, please put me at the right place so that i can flourish.

11. I have realized that I need to create my own empire to smother their bullshit.

Detachment Is Must

12. People? Nope... I want to rule the sky.

13. An attachment is a virus that eats you up from within.

14. My shadow want to guide and shriek about the right path but it has no voice.

15. Enough. Don't chase anything which is fetching your inner peace.

Ayushi Bhatnagar

Ayushi Bhatnagar is currently pursuing her undergraduate degree of medicine from Kalinga Institute of Medical Sciences. She is skilled in writing, sketching as well as in photography. Her writing skills may be confirmed on Instagram and Facebook page named KARAVAAN. She specially enjoys listening to other people's stories, be it sad or happy. Her writings express her own experiences and stories which most of us can relate to

ममता

यूं तो तेरी ममता की तारीफ सब करते हैं
यूं तो सबको दिखता है तेरा दर्द
यूं तो सब समझना चाहते हैं तुझे
यूं तो राह दिखा कर पीछे खड़ी रहती है

यूं तो हंस कर यही कह देती है मैं ठीक हूं
यूं तो सब की खुशी में ही तो खुश हो जाती है
यूं तो अपनी रूहानियत से सब में जान भर देती है
तो सबसे खूबसूरत इनायत है

मगर तेरी पहचान तेरी खुद से है
तेरे मां होने से नहीं" "

Fire Within Me

Flood of my gushing blood
Vanished all that i had
Winds, that could have been stopped
Rushed through my mouth
The crack that i hid with my rack
Should have been packed
Amidst the situations of bewilderness,
It was my guilted soul that I stacked."

जिंदगानी है या शतरंज

यह कागज का टुकड़ा है, या है यह एक कहानी,
साहिल की तलाश सिपाही को है, या फतेह की राह तुम्हारी,
बचना बचाना है राजा को या ईमान की करें रखवाली,
इन प्यादो की यही चाल है, या मंसूबा तुम्हारी,
खेल जीतने की शिद्दत है या है यही कहानी
खेल खेलते हम शतरंज का या है यह जिंदगानी"

Shipra S Gupta

"Shipra is the Founder of www.hijindgi.com
She lives in Delhi NCR with her husband and children.
She is a blogger, writer and Poetess.
Her Favourite job is the one she is doing now full time writing.
If you want to know more about her kindly visit her website
www.hijindgi.com"

जिंदगी का सफ़र

जिंदगी का सफ़र कभी आसान नहीं हुआ करता। हमेशा अलग-अलग अनुभवों से भरा होता है। आज मै आपको अपनी जिंदगी के उन्ही पन्नों से रूबरू कराती हूँ।

उन दिनों मै बंगलौर में रहती थी। रहती तो परिवार के साथ ही थी पर वो साथ कभी अपना होकर भी अपना नहीं था। सब अंजाने अजनबियों की तरह अपने - अपने खोल में सिमटे हुए।

मैं भी पूरे घर का काम निपटाते हुए एक गृहिणी की भूमिका निभा रही थी। अपने आपको पूरी तरह से भूल चुकी थी कि मेरा भी कोई अस्तितव् है।

उन्ही दिनों अचानक घर के सामने वाले घर में हलचल दिखने लगी। एक युवती, उसका छोटा बच्चा और पति। छोटी सी सुखी जिंदगी।

धीरे- धीरे युवती जिसका नाम नीरू था।, मुझ से बातें करने लगी और मैं जब भी समय मिलता उसके घर जाती। हम एक दूसरे से बहुत बातें करते थे। वो मेरे लिए बिल्कुल मेरी छोटी बहन जैसी बन चुकी थी।

नीरू ने एम. एस. सी.गणित से की हुई थी और वो घर पर ही बच्चो को पढ़ाती भी थी।

एक दिन मै उसके घर पर ही थी कि तभी एक बच्चा उस से हिंदी में कुछ पूछने लगा। नीरू के बोलने से पहले ही मैं ने जवाब दे दिया। नीरू ने कहा "दीदी आपकी हिंदी इतनी अच्छी है आप किसी स्कूल में क्यों नहीं पढ़ा लेती"? मुझे बड़ा आश्चर्य हुआ क्योकि मैं ने ये कभी नहीं सोचा था।

घर में सभी के विरोध करने के बावजूद, पूरे घर के काम की जिम्मेदारी का भरोसा दिलाते हुए मैं ने एक स्कूल में नौकरी करनी शुरू कर दी।

अब स्कूल जाने के लिए किसी साधन की भी जरूरत थी। नीरू ने मुझे स्कूटी लेने के लिए प्रेरित किया और उसके साथ जाकर मैं ने एक स्कूटी भी ले ली, फिर स्कूटी सिखाने की जिम्मेदारी भी उसने खुद लेते हुए मुझे सुबह के समय स्कूटी भी सिखाई।

नीरू ने मुझे फिर से एक नई जिंदगी जीने का रास्ता दिखाया। जो कि अनवरत कई सालों तक चलता रहा। उसके पति का तबादला दिल्ली हो गया। वो दिल्ली चली गई।

नीरू ने मुझे जिस नई जिंदगी को जीने की प्रेरणा दी ,वो आज तक मुझ में है। मैं अपनी जिंदगी को यू ही जी रही थी बिना किसी उद्देश्य के, आज मेरे पास उद्देश्य भी है।

मैं और नीरू आज भी एक अच्छी बहनो की तरह मिलते है फिर से उसी जोश और उमंग के साथ अपने सुख- दुःख बाँटते है। नीरू आज भी मेरे लिए उतना ही सोचती है और बड़ी बहन की तरह प्यार करती है।

हाँ! मैं ये मानती हूँ कि अगर नीरू मेरी जिंदगी में नहीं आती तो मेरी जिंदगी में इतना सुकून और कुछ कर गुजरने की इच्छा भी नहीं आती।

तुम्हारा बहुत- बहुत धन्यवाद नीरू।

Sakshi Singh

Sakshi Singh from Korba, C.G. is a 1st professional MBBS student and she considers literature, colours and music as her best companion.

ज़िंदगी : एहसास बचपन का"

वो काग़ज़ की कश्ती और नदियों का पानी,
वो मिट्टी के खिलौने और राजा रानी की कहानी,
आज कुछ नादानियां बाहर निकाली हैं मैंने जेब टटोल कर...

उन फ़ुरसत के रंगों को छोड़ व्यस्त दुनिया में कदम रखा है,
ख़ुद को पहचान दिलाने ज़िम्मेदारी तले बचपन दफ़न कर...

हर सहर उस रोशनी का इंतज़ार,
बस्ते का बोझ फिर सुकून भरा इतवार,
उन हर झगड़ों का इस तारीख पर मुकदमा चाहूं,
मुझे तो ये भी याद नहीं कि भूला क्या हूं?

आज लौट आई हैं आंखों में चमक उन जज़्बातों के तूफान के कारण,
बिखर गई हैं यादें सारी इस सांझ की दीवार पर..."

एक पहेली : स्त्री"

उसके लाख मना करने पर भी तुम दरिंदों की तरह पेश आओगे,
पर कोई बात नहीं....
'वो स्त्री है', तुम्हारी खुशियों के लिए सहेगी भी....

इस चार दीवारी में क़ैद रहने के बावजूद आवाम उस पर लांछन भी लगाएगी,
पर कोई बात नहीं....
'वो स्त्री है', चुपचाप सर पर आंचल संभाले फिर से सपने बुनेगी भी.....

बेतहाशा तुम उसकी कमियां निकालोगे कि रोटी सूख गई या नमक कम है,
पर फिर भी कोई बात नहीं....
'वो स्त्री है' हताश है तो क्या हुआ, तुम्हारी प्यास बुझाने वो बहेगी भी.....

और अगर तुम्हारी ज़िंदगी में कभी अंधेरा छा भी जाए न तो घबराना नहीं,
'वो स्त्री है', तुम्हारी ज़िंदगी रोशन करने के लिए जलेगी भी....

"वक़्त, छल और ज़िंदगी"

ज़िंदगी के इस दौर का बेशक मुझे कोई मलाल नहीं,
छल से भरपूर इंसान हैं उनसे भी कोई सवाल नहीं...

हो कोई जो मुझे ज़िंदगी के सफल मायने बताए,
सबका मददगार बनूं ऐसा संभव कराए...

इस ज़िंदगी से परे मेरा एक अलग संसार हो,
जहां हर दर्द के हमदर्द हों और खुशियों से आभार हो...

हो कोई जो मुझे ज़हर सुधा का फर्क बताए,
द्वेष भूल निस्वार्थ प्रेम का अर्क बताए...

मैं मुन्तज़िर हूं उस पल का जब आए वो मेरी दहलीज़ लांघ कर,
बेशर्त मैं उसे साहिल पार कराऊं इस संसार के सारे अहंकार हार कर...

"मैं बादल बन जाऊं"

फरेब की धूप से झुलस गई ज़मीर अगर अश्क से धुल सकती है,
तो उन उम्मीद भरे अश्कों का मैं बादल बन जाऊं...

भले ही यूं दर्द ने बार बार दस्तक दी हो तुम्हारी दहलीज़ पर,
तुम्हारी खुशियां समेट कर काश उन खुशियों का मैं काजल बन जाऊं...

Nishant Kamble

"Nishant Kamble is a poet, shayar and author who writes from his experience of life. He believes in making the reader imagine life in few stanzas. Humor being his favourite, try and read the emotions between the lines.

He is a 27 years old MBA in Finance from Mumbai who is also good at dancing, acting, singing & sports, but for some reason, he is still single.

To read more of his content you can follow his Instagram handle @kai_unkahi_baaten or if you want to just stalk him, follow @nishant_bittu77"

दोस्त मेरा भी एक है..

लौंडा वो भी बडा सख्त था,
लेकिन आब गुज़र चुका वो वक़्त था...
दिल उसका भी नेक था,
दोस्त मेरा भी एक था...

पहले साथ में रहा करते थे,
तो ज़िन्दगी भी हंसने पर मजबुर थी ...
आब इतनी बात नहीं होती,
मुलाकात ??? वो तो बहुत दुर थी...

सात साल की दोस्ती को मैंने,
अपन यार का नाम दीया...
और दो दीन की हिमाकत को उसने,
अपने प्यार का नाम दिया...

दोस्ती शायद सिर्फ मैंने की थी,
उसने सिर्फ प्यार था किया...
फिर आख़िर में उसने,
मेरी दोस्ती को हीं, धोखा था दिया...

हज़ारो की भीड थीं कॉलेज में,
फिर भी मुझे उसी में सच्चा दोस्त दिख गया...
आब वो झूठे बहाने बनके अपनी बंदी से मिलने जात है,
पता नहीं, मुझसे झूठ बोलना वो कब सीख गया...

खाना तो वो रोज़ खाती थी,
बीमार मैं भी कभी रेहता था,

फिर भी, ""मेरे बाबू ने खाना खाया ?"" वो रोज पुछता,
पर, ""दोस्त तूने दवाई ली?"" उसने कभी नहीं पुछा...

वो डिस्को में उसके साथ शराब पीएगा,
फेसबुक पर फोटो के साथ चेक-इन करेगा...
मैं उसपर भी दिल वाला रिएक्ट करूंगा,
और तन्हाई का दर्द अकेले ही सहूंगा...

रातभर जागकर, उसके असाइनमेंट मैं लिखता,
इंटरव्यू उसका हो तो, तैयारी मैं करता...
फ़िर भी वो कहता, ""मेरे प्यार का रिश्ता ही अलग हैं""
आख़िर मुझे भी पता चला, ""अकले फिल्म देखने का मजा भी अलग है...""

मुझसे बात करने वाला अब कोई नहीं है,
फ़िर भी देर रात तक जागता हूं...
आब आप पुछोगे, ""जाग कर करता क्या है?""
मेरे यारो... ये सब उन्हीं लम्हों में तो लिखा गया हैं...

मुझे तो फ्लर्ट करना नहीं आता,
लगत है, अकेला ही मारूंगा...
वो भले मेरी दोस्ती का इस्तेमाल करे, मैं उसपर नहीं रुठुंगा,
क्योंकी उसके लिए, मैं अच्छा था, अच्छा हूं और अच्छा हीं रूहंगा..."

अच्छा लगता है

ज़िन्दगी में ऐसा कोई हो,
तो अच्छा लगत है...

खाना खिलाने वाला ना सही,
"पर खाना खाया या नहीं ?"
ये पूछने वाला कोई हो...
तो अच्छा लगत है...

गोद में सर रख कर सुलाने वाला ना सही,
"पर मैं नींद से जाग पाया या नहीं ?"
ये जानने वाला कोई हो...
तो अच्छा लगत है...

खयाल रखने वाला ना सही,
"पर दवई ली या नहीं ?"
ये देखने वाला कोई हो...
तो अच्छा लगत है...

दिन भर बात करने वला ना सही,
पर सोने से पहले "दिन कैसा गया ?"
ये पूछने वाला कोई हो...
तो अच्छा लगत है...

मेरी तरक्की की दुआ करने वाला ना सही,
"पर मैं जैसा रहूं खुश रहूं",

ये चाहने वाला कोई हो...
तो अच्छा लगत है...

मैं रूठूं तो मनाने वाला ना सही,
"पर मैं रूठा हूं,"
ये पहचानने वाला कोइ हो...
तो अच्छा लगत है...

जनम का रिश्ता निभाने वाला ना सही,
"पर मैं उसका अपना हूं",
ये जताने वाला कोई हो...
तो अच्छा लगत है...

हर मोड़ पर साथ निभाने वाला ना सही,
"पर रास्ता पार करते समय",
ये हाथ थामने वाला कोई हो...
तो अच्छा लगत है...

मेरी गलती सुधारने वाला ना सही,
"पर गलात और सही में क्या फरक है ?"
ये समझाने वाला कोई हो...
तो अच्छा लगत है...

गिरते हुए आंसू पूछने वाला ना सही,
"पर दिल को तसल्ली दिला कर",
कांधे पर हाथ रखने वाला कोई हो...

तो अच्छा लगत है...

ईद पर बिरियानी खिलाने वाला ना सही,
"पर इफ्तारी के वक़्त अपने खाने का एक हिस्सा आगे बढ़ा कर",
रोजा सफ़ल कराने वाला कोई हो,
तो अच्छा लगत है...

Richa Rohit Gupta

रिश्तों को अपनी ज़िन्दगी का आधार मानती हैं और दिल में कुछ बड़ा कर दिखाने का जुनून और होंसला रखती हैं।

यह हैं ऋचा रोहित गुप्ता। यह दिल्ली की रहने वाली हैं जो पेशे से एक अध्यापिका हैं।इनकी रसायन शास्त्र और मनोविज्ञान विषयों में गहरी रुचि है। खुद को जानने और अभिव्यक्त करने के लिए ये लेखन को सबसे उपयुक्त माध्यम मानती हैं। इन्हें सामाजिक मुद्दों और संवेदनशील विषयों पर लिखना पसंद है।

'Always love, laugh and smile-no matter what' is the mantra of her life.

एहसास - वक़्त की रेत पर

"बीते वक़्त की धुंधली यादों ने
ना जाने कितने एहसास दिए
किन - किन को बयां करूं मै
शायद अल्फ़ाज़ भी कम पड़ें
तो क्या हुआ कुछ खट्टे थे, कुछ मीठे भी तो थे
जो खट्टे थे वो ज़िन्दगी के सबब दे गए
और जो मीठे थे, वो जीने की वज़ह बने"

जी हां दोस्तों हम सबकी ज़िन्दगी कहीं ना कहीं कुछ कहे अनकहे एहसासों की ही कड़ी है और यह एहसास ही होते हैं जो हमारे आने वाले कल की दिशा निर्धारित करते हैं।

बस कुछ ऐसा ही मेरे साथ भी हुआ।यह बात उन दिनों की है जब मैं दिल्ली के एक नामी स्कूल में पढ़ाया करती थी।मेरा रिश्ता पक्का हो चुका था और शादी में लगभग छह महीने का वक्त था।सब कुछ अच्छा चल रहा था।मेरे होने वाले पति और ससुराल वाले भी काफी खुश थे।

फिर अचानक से मेरी ज़िंदगी में एक ऐसा मोड़ आया जिसने कुछ वक़्त के लिए सब कुछ बदल कर रख दिया।

गर्मियों की छुट्टियां होने वाली थी।हमारे स्कूल की प्रिंसिपल ने आखिरी हफ्ते में मुझे बुलाया और कहा कि अगला सेशन शुरू होने से पहले आपको हमारे पैनल के सामने इंटरव्यू देने के लिए आना है।उनकी ये बात सुनकर मुझे बहुत बुरा लगा।और इसके कई कारण भी थे।

बच्चे मेरे पढ़ाने के ढंग से काफी प्रभावित थे।वो रसायन शास्त्र (जो मेरा विषय है) समझने में रुचि लेने लगे थे।इस कारण उस साल हमारा बोर्ड रिज़ल्ट भी सबसे अच्छा रहा।मुझे रसायन शास्त्र

डिपार्टमेंट का हैड बना दिया गया।मेरी ज्वाइनिंग के एक साल के अंदर ही मैनेजमेंट ने मुझे पूरी सैलरी (गर्वनमेंट ग्रेड) भी देनी शुरू कर दी...

उस वक़्त मन में एक ही सवाल तंग कर रहा था...सब कुछ तो ठीक चल रहा है, तो फिर दुबारा ये इंटरव्यू क्यों?

शायद उस वक़्त मै इतनी समझदार नहीं थी कि इन व्यावसायिक बातों को समझ सकूं। मेरे मन में एक अजीब सा अहम था कि जब सब मुझसे इतने खुश हैं तो मेरी जगह वहां कोई नहीं ले सकता।बस यही सब सोचकर मै इंटरव्यू देने नहीं गई।

कुछ दिनों बाद छुट्टियों में मुझे स्कूल बुलाया गया और मुझे पता चलता है कि क्योंकि मै उनके कहे अनुसार इंटरव्यू देने के लिए नहीं पहुंची , इसलिए उन्होंने मेरी जगह किसी और को नियुक्त कर लिया है।(हालांकि जो कुछ भी हुआ, प्रिंसिपल ने उसे अपनी मज़बूरी बताकर खेद भी जताया और सांत्वना स्वरूप आने वाले वक़्त में मुझसे संपर्क में रहने को भी कहा)।
पर यह सब मेरे लिए कुछ ऐसा था जैसे पांव तले ज़मीन खिसक गई हो।अपने परिवार को होने वाली परेशानियों से ज्यादा मुझे अपने ससुराल वालों की चिंता हो रही थी कि वो लोग क्या सोचेंगे, क्या कहेंगे(क्योंकि हमारे समाज में अमूमन हर रिश्ते की बुनियाद मनपसंद खानदान के साथ कहीं ना कहीं आपके होने वाले साथी की अच्छी नौकरी और सैलरी भी होती है)।

मन में चल रही इन सब बातों के साथ मै जैसे - तैसे अपने आंसुओं को छुपाए नज़दीकी मेट्रो स्टेशन पहुंच गई।इतने में तेज़ बारिश शुरू हो गई। अच्छा ही हुआ क्योंकि उस बारिश कि बूंदों में मै अपने दिल

के दर्द को बहते हुए आंसुओं के साथ कुछ कम करने की कोशिश कर रही थी।

मै करीब दो घंटे मेट्रो स्टेशन पर अकेले एक कोने में बैठी रही। मन में ढेरों सवाल चल रहे थे कि मम्मी - पापा सब कुछ कैसे संभालेंगे, मेरे ससुराल वाले कहीं रिश्ता तो नहीं तोड़ देंगे?यही सोचते - सोचते मैंने हिम्मत करके अपने होने वाले पति को फ़ोन किया और सब बात बताई।उस वक़्त तो उन्होंने कुछ खास नहीं कहा, बस मुझे मिलने के लिए बुलाया।

मै उसी तेज़ बारिश में उनसे मिलने गई।मेरे आंसुओं और बारिश की बूंदों ने मुझे पूरी तरह भिगो दिया था। वो आए और आते ही उन्होंने मुझे प्यार से अपने पास बिठाया।इससे पहले कि मै कुछ बोल पाती उन्होंने अपना हाथ मेरे होठों पर रखा और कहा - आपको कुछ कहने और समझाने की जरूरत नहीं है।फिर मेरा हाथ अपने हाथ में लेकर बोले - मै हूं ना आपके साथ।हम दोनों मिलकर कुछ ना कुछ हल निकाल लेंगे। बेशक अभी हमारी शादी नहीं हुई है पर मैंने दिल से आपको अपना जीवन - साथी उसी दिन मान लिया था जब हमारा रोका हुआ था। ये रिश्ता अब जब हम दोनों को मिलकर निभाना है, तो फिर कोई भी परेशानी या तकलीफ़ आप अकेले क्यों झेलेंगी?

उनके इतना कहते ही मेरे मन में चल रहा तूफ़ान आंसू बन झर - झर बह निकला और एक डरी सहमी सी लड़की सारी शर्म - लिहाज़ छोड़ उनकी बाहों में चली गई।

उस दिन मेरे होने वाले पति के वो शब्द ही काफी थे मुझे ये एहसास दिलाने के लिए की रिश्ता चाहे कोई भी हो,उसमे रूहानियत जरूरी है। हम कहां किस मुकाम पर हैं , ये इतना मायने नहीं रखता।वास्तव

में ये रिश्ते ही ज़िन्दगी में सफलता के मानक हैं जिन्हें कुछ शब्दों में अभिव्यक्त नहीं किया जा सकता।
और पति पत्नी के रिश्ते से ज्यादा खूबसूरत तो भला क्या ही होगा, जो खून की बूंदों से जुड़े नहीं हैं, जिनकी परवरिश और ज़िन्दगी को देखने का नजरिया अलग है, पर फिर भी सात फेरों में बंधकर पूरी ज़िन्दगी गुज़ार देते हैं एक दूसरे की खुशी के लिए।

आज हमें एक दूसरे से जुड़े हुए लगभग दस साल हो चुके हैं।इस बीच हमने कई उतार - चड़ाव भी देखे।पर हर बार वो (मेरे पति) एक मज़बूत आधार स्तंभ की तरह मेरे साथ खड़े रहे ।

दोस्तों, आज बेशक मै अपने क्षेत्र में काफी आगे निकल चुकी हूं। पढ़ाने का जो सफर मात्र एक नौकरी के रूप में शुरू हुआ था, वो अब मेरी ज़िन्दगी का हिस्सा बन चुका है।मेरी अब यही कोशिश रहती है कि मैंने जो कुछ भी सिखा है, जाना है उसे मै उन गरीब बच्चों तक भी पहुंचा पाऊं जिनमें सीखने की लगन तो है पर साथ ही अपनी मंज़िल तक पहुंचने के लिए किसी सहारे की भी जरूरत है।

पर एक सच ये भी है कि वक़्त की उस मार ने मुझे ज़िन्दगी का सबसे बड़ा सबक सिखा दिया और वो ये कि चाहे आप कितने ही काबिल और किसी के प्यारे क्यों ना हो,आपकी जगह कभी भी कोई भी ले सकता है।
और साथ ही ये एहसास भी कराया कि रिश्तों की खूबसूरती उनकी सच्चाई में है और ऐसे रिश्ते किसी भी अभाव की पूर्ति का पर्याय बन सकते हैं।

Sakshi Sehrawat

"Sakshi Sehrawat is a graduate in physics and a writer by heart. She finds poetry as a way to connect to the soul. She believes words have the power to heal any soul or even to kill one, so should always be chosen very wisely. She loves to write and words are her best friend. She believes appreciation helps a person to develop and tries to give her best at everything she does. She enjoys expressing herself through poetries. She wishes to spend her life in service for the nation. She has participated in numerous writing contests and also won a few of them. The aim of her life is to have some positive impact on the society and would find herself fortunate enough if she could change at least one life positively.
Find her writings @words__can__heal_ on Instagram."

जीवन एक सपना

कुछ उम्मीदों का सामान सजा के,
हौंसलों की उड़ान हम भर चले।
जो अरमान रखे थे दिल में छिपा के
आज वो भी जीने की आशा करने लगे।

ममता के आंचल की छाँव में,
पिता के कंधों की सवारी पर,
ढूँढते खुद को उनकी परछाई में,
यूँ बीत गया बचपन का सफ़र।

दोस्तों के साथ मस्ती करते
नादानी भरे उलाहने देकर,
किसी अनजानी राह पर चलते
ज़िन्दगी मंज़िल तलाशने ही लगी मगर।

कुछ ठोकर जो लगीं हमें फिर,
एक नयी रोशनी दिखाने लगी।
जीवन लगा यूँ जैसे सपनों का हो असर
हर मुश्किल कुछ नया सिखाने लगी।

Dreamy Shady Reality

I was having a lovely sleep,
when suddenly I opened my eyes.
Into a new world of belief
and found my mother beside.

It was a happy new morning,
all my loved ones were around me.
I gathered a lot of blessings
and thought the world was lovely.

But then came the noon time
and I was exposed to the world.
Life then became somewhat like lime
and it was becoming a curl.

When my day reached the afternoon,
I realized it was a bit late.
I had to recognise myself soon,
As none had the time to wait.

In the evening my friends were away,
I missed them to much extent.
I had a lot to express and say,
But none was able to understand.

Finally the night arrived,
which was the destination.
Life decided to sleep tight
And I praised mine as the awesome one."

Miss My Home When Away

I used to get up early in the morning,
then I do these days.
I used to get frequent but sweet warning,
I will remember always.

Maa told me everyday,
to take care in every way.
Every little word she told daily
and the ones she told specially.
All I remember, all I miss,
How she helped me through justice.

Papa told me everyday,
to be brave in every way.
Though he did not speak much,
his silence also gave a blessing touch.
I want that life back again
when he was there in all the pain.

Brother told me everyday,
to remain happy in every way.
He fought with me over little matters, remembering even the
fights, my heart scatters.
I still love to tease him,
sharing with him my life dream.

Yes, the life was beautiful,
extremely adorable
at home,
where lies my heart and soul.

Bhagyasree. G

Bhagyasree, is a budding poet who writes nature based poems. She is inspired by her immediate surroundings for writing poetry. Her writings also include short stories and articles published in college magazines.

Hill Rider

Hills are the most beautiful place for a long drive may it be with friends or lovers. Riding up the hill gives the whole heart an over whelming joy while admiring the flowery boughs, green hues and a pricking wind gliding down in hush. The dusk is bright with the pretty red and orange sky shading itself in the horizon. You might be a king in skating in the plains, for hours and far distances but here in the hills, you slip away among the huge mountains or slip down a little valley, if you just lend your eye for a minute.

I'm proud to say that I am the daughter of the Queen of hills, residing here for twenty years. I have grown with these trees, imbibing all the love they gave me, running down the streams often and once, I have learnt to ride, I live with nature.

If you are lucky enough to drive in a Royal Enfield that's great, but I'm happy with the white Activa that flies quite well. Wearing a thick doubled layer green jack, that's absolutely waterproof and a black mask over the nose is most requisite to enjoy the drive. I start in the early morning, through the narrow blind curves. Every curve is a surprise but more than that it's dangerous. You drive with an anticipation without being clear of what is actually coming. It can be a slow vehicle coming down, or a cow just happily crossing, or even at times a dog just jumping out the bush. It happens to me often when I am in a rush and I tend to get stuck behind buses and moreover unable to take over through the narrow road.

But then, when I decide to take a short cut through the forest, it is a total adventure on the whole. There is no warmth of the sun, it's only the wet moss all over and slippery mud. The boughs are too low, touching the eye, irritating at times.

Inspite of all this, driving through the hills is an awesome feeling. You feel yourself one with the nature, in the depths of green and brown, with pretty leaves and flowers. There are no buildings, no human at times and even no noises. I see the footprints of the bison or the Lion tailed macaque. Malabar giant squirrel looks attractive and very enthusiastically jumping on the trees.

There are long stretches of trees grown just like a hulk with heavy branches spreading all over. In the winter times, they sit happily over the mountains covered by the ice that slowly flows down in the dawn. Every hill rider escapes the town and drive far across the forest borders trying to experience something new, beautiful than what generally seems to be. The best part is, people cannot walk steadily, they just reel through the forest as they step on uneven landscape.

The clouds are filled with life, with vibrant colours drawing across the sky in distinct forms.

Once it so happened, my brother and I walked into the most isolated forest. Picking up leaves of different shades of green, and pines, we got separated. Only after a little while, I myself realized. The place seemed haunting and I had no one to call out for help. I ran and ran looking out for the place I saw my bro at last, and I reached the place finally by identifying the leaves I had kept collecting in an order. It's an unforgettable experience ever.

I just hope that in the years to come, the beauty and peace of my place remains imperishable.

Bridal Makeup

Pastries are the most delicious, most delicate,
To be held as soft as neonate's hand,
They just slip away between your fingers,
That you might never take notice of!

You can bake them well,
And relish the smell,
But the labour you take to decorate them,
Takes more time than a bride!

The initial cream spread over it,
Seems mere patchworks done,
And then adding to them a few colours,
Just to make them look fluffy and bright.

A few toppings of jelly assorted,
Topping of chocolate cigar,
And then, a few roses made,
Covering the patched edges!

But yes, once it is done,
It's a perfect bride,
That suddenly became beautiful,
Just for a little while.

Aysha Nihidha

A student in mathematics, loves to express herself through poetry, trying to escape from real world using her imagination.

Letting It Go Forever

Being only ten, was I supposed to know ?
To understand what was happening !
The one needed to guide me
Was the one who lead me to it !

I asked you a glass of advice,
You poured me negative thoughts !
I asked you to feed me love,
You fed me your depression !

For desert you gave me mental torture,
I had no proof to show to people,
As physical torture was only evident !
Mental torture never existed in society.

My only hope was social media,
I felt I can be something,
By seeking negative attention on social media !
People did praise me there !

All was good, One day suddenly,
Hate comments appeared, I wondered
Did I do something wrong ? Nah, because
People supported me trashing haters !

I was only ten, I didn't know,
I can't ask, wait whom can I ask ?
I was lost in sea of desperation,
Social media attention was my safe shore.

Years later I realize, what I did !
But no why I did ! Why did I do it ?
Is it because of mental torture ? Or neglection ?
Or misguiding social media posts ?

It has become traumas now,haunting me

When I talk, adults claim it's just a phase of teenage
Life, justifying by saying they suffered more, Maybe
These would be better if someone had listen to all of us.

I was only ten, is my act justified ?
I kept on asking ? No, Maybe not...
I kept on answering those,
I had started hating myself, taunting myself.....

Traumas haunted me , everyday,
Keeping me awake at night,
Keeping me disturbed at day,
Many seasons passed traumas increased.

I deal with hard feelings,
Self harm was my healer,
Was I justified ? Who cares ? Sadly,
I am just in phase of teenage, I reminisced.

Years later on, grown adult I had become,
I understand, It wasn't my fault,
I did my best, nor could change anything,
I forgive myself now, preaching self love !

Was it my fault really ? Not exactly dear,
Was my act justified ? Yes my dear,
All these nightmare of questions, seems long lost,
As I don't live in my past anymore !
Letting it go forever..."

Letter To Myself

(A poem written in form of letter, reconnect past experience of life)

To,
Younger me,
lost somewhere in past

Date: Sometime in future

From
Older me,
Stuck somewhere in present

Dear me,
Where are you?
I miss you, I miss us,
Do you remember the time when
we where innocent?
Do you remember the time when
candy made us happy?
Do you remember the time when
we had hearty laughs?
Do you remember the time when
we got sad and cried?
Do you remember the time when
we got angry and remained silent?
Do you remember the time when
life was simple and fun?

Come back soon, please....

Yours Lovingly
Yourself"

Annu Singh

Am from delhi currently working at BPCL. I penned down my feelings which I unable to share.

गुड़ वन

किसी के लिए दिल में भड़ास रखके क्या कर लोगे आप
वह जितना हंसेगा इतनी आपको तकलीफ होगी
तो इस से अच्छा है कि किसी की खुशी में खुश हो जाओ
क्या पता आपको इससे खुशी मिले या ना मिले
लेकिन उसकी खुशी से आप खुश हो जाओ"   "जिंदगी

कभी हस आएगी कभी रुलाएगी
औरों की मदद करा कर खुशी भी देगी
कभी अपनी मदद के लिए आंसू भी देगी

यह जिंदगी है यार
या रोना भी पड़ेगा
यहां लड़ना भी पड़ेगा
कभी समझाना भी पड़ेगा
कभी अपनों को
कभी गैरों को
कभी खुद को"

सफ़र ए जिंदगी

नहीं मिलता कोई बिना मतलब के
इस जिंदगानी के सफर में
कोई अपना हिसाब करने आता है
तो कोई अपना कर्ज चुकाने

कर्मों का खेल चलता ही रहता है साथ
इस जन्म में या अगले जन्म में
कभी ना कभी करता ही है हिसाब"

Ritwika Ghosh

Ritwika Ghosh, born on August 2, 1997, belongs to a Bengali family. She lives in Kolkata, West Bengal. She loves to write poetries. She is an English Hons. graduated student from Calcutta University. Writing poems on various theme is her passion.

Life

Life is like a rollercoaster,
Don't treat it like a bread in a toaster.
It is a cup of wine,
A sum which always shines.
It is a gift of God.
So soon don't get bored.
Enjoy it but take care of injunctions.
It brings both train of happiness and sadness on its railway junction.
It will give you a chance and say let your mistake hide,
But for this never commit suicide.

WHAT IS LIFE?

Life is a mystery.
Interesting like Chemistry.
Boring like Physics.
Without any lyrics.
Puzzling like Mathematics.
Dear like Statistics.
With an angle in Geometry.
And sleepy like History.
Lovely like English.
Hard as a muddle.
And unknown like a puzzle.

The Truth Of Life

A joker says life is funny
A rich man says life is money
A beggar says life is a struggle
A wise man says life is a puzzle
A lazy man says life is meant for laziness
A youngster says life is full of pleasure
A saint says life is the way to reach God
But oh Almighty!
I think life is an unsolved mystery.

Pradeep Sengar

"He is alumni of Aligarh Muslim University.he did engineering in Electronics & communication.he did teaching in various engineering colleges. he is working in Aviation industry.

He likes to play chess, travelling historical places,watching black & white movies.
he is writing in hindi.he loved brajabhasha.his poems published in various magzines."
Instagrsm :
pinklotussengar
Twitter: @PinklotusSengar
Facebook:
https://www.facebook.com/Pradeep-Sengar
490983398021270/

क़त्लगाह

करे हुकूमत,दिलों की सल्तनत पे
वो हर अजीज , बादशाह कहाँ है

पढ़ें जाएँ खुतबे, गरीब नवाज के
बता दे मुझे, वो खानकाह कहाँ है

शाम होते ही, जो होती थी रौनक़
महफिलों में वो, वाह-वाह कहाँ है

सच बोलने का, जो दम भरते थे
कहो तो मुद्दई , वो गवाह कहाँ है

मर मिटने को, जो तैयार हो गए
इश्क के मारे, वो तबाह कहाँ है

जख्मों पे मरहम, ऐसे लगाया तूने
मालूम न चला, वो कराह कहाँ है

जहाँ रिश्तों को,खत्म किया जाता
ऐ मेरे हमदम,वो कत्लगाह कहाँ है

नमक

मेरे सर मढ़ दिए तूने अपने गुनाह
कुबूल क्यों न की तूने मेरी चाह
दर्द उठता है अब तुम्हारे सीने में कैसा लगता है मेरे बिन जीने में
खता तेरी थी या था बहुत मजबूर
किसलिए मुझसे हो गया तू दूर
आज हम दोनों, फिर से इक बार
चलो, वही काम पुराना करते हैं
इक दूजे के जख्मों पर
फिर से नमक छिड़कते हैं

(3)

और क्या चाहिए
साँस लेने को जैसे हवा चाहिए
ठीक होने को जैसे दवा चाहिए
है हसरत हमारी बस इतनी सनम
मिल जाय तू तो और क्या चाहिए

दिल धड़कता है अब तो जोरों से
ना मिला कर तू गली के छोरों से
है हसरत हमारी बस इतनी सनम
तू हम से मिले और क्या चाहिए...

न गुजरते हैं दिन न कटती हैं रातें
ख्यालों में तुझसे हम करते हैं बातें
है हसरत हमारी बस इतनी सनम
हम तुझ से मिलें और क्या चाहिए

सुना है बहुत हैं तेरे चाहने वाले
मगर ना होंगे हम जैसे दिलवाले
है हसरत हमारी बस इतनी सनम
तू हमको चाहे और क्या चाहिए

बंद पलकों में बस तेरा ख्वाब है
मेरे सारे सवालों का तू जवाब है
है हसरत हमारी बस इतनी सनम
तेरे ख्वाबों में रहूँ और क्या चाहिए

मेरे हाथों में बस इक तेरा हाथ हो

जाँ जब तक रहे बस तेरा साथ हो
है हसरत हमारी बस इतनी सनम
उम्रभर संग रहें और क्या चाहिए

इस जग में हम, कल रहें न रहें
सब हमारे तराने, गुनगुनाते रहें
है हसरत हमारी बस इतनी सनम
मरकर भी जिएँ और क्या चाहिए

#औरक्याचाहिए

Anupama Das

Anupama Das is a Kolkata based Mental Health Enthusiast with a Master's Degree in Psychology. She is also a certified Graphologist. She loves talking to strangers and meeting new people. She is incredibly passionate about food and also has a food blog on Instagram (@ds_anupama). She has an above-average knowledge about fashion and also appreciates her relationships to be transparent and organic.

Fit In Or Stand Out?

Sometimes life can be so tricky that it almost becomes impossible to survive; to go on increasing your patience to get to somewhere secure and stable. I feel we make it more tormenting by trying to fit into what our society makes us believe is correct and bearing instead of making the youth recognize their ability to belong to something.

Some people consciously choose to fit in even though they belong to a different world but that world seems like fiction to them; a world which provides them the luxury to be whom they are truly made for. It does not mean that the values, virtues, and beliefs of our ancestors and heritage become any less important but every individual is blessed with a gift which they need to explore to present the world with their innovation. The notion of the hunger for social recognition has always prevailed in our society since forever. What made me wonder is that why are we so obsessed with the validation of our surrounding? Our passion and ambition hold the strength to overpower the disapproval of society. Maybe people think that disapproving someone's dream would demoralize them to pursue their own journey. But the most satirical fact is that with this disapproval comes the freedom of action which serves as a blessing for dreamers. A prolonged disapproval results in giving up which makes us free from the burden of other's expectations; the only expectation we have to meet is our owns.

Fitting in cannot always be the ultimate solution for bringing peace. Sometimes a storm is necessary to make us realize the difference between necessity and luxury. There comes a point when breaking the barrier is no longer a luxury but it becomes necessary to stand out and define what we are and what we can be. Does fitting in makes any sense when it makes you question your existence? This battle comes with its risks and at times can take away chunks of our regular surroundings but eventually, it always makes us stronger for the journey we have set for ourselves. At the end of the day, you will always be glad for taking the initiative of making an effort to belong to your fiction and making it your reality.

I think it necessary to take charge of your journey which is solely chosen and defined by your gut and when you do that it is standard to find yourself in a state of discomfort. But before you know it this discomfort deepens your conviction to achieve your final goal and facilitates you to thrive to bring the best in you. When you feel like you are already there where you wanted to be you find yourself stepping onto your next adventure. What we need to realize is that our lives are an everlasting process of becoming and belonging to oneself. Wasting our time and energy to fit in reflects in shortening this amusing ride.

Abhilash Rout

"Abhilash Rout is from Cuttack, Odisha.
He has completed his graduation in B.Com with Accounts Honours.
He is preparing for competitive exams too. He has been working for the welfare of working out for the weaker sections of the society.
Writing has been a part of expressing his feelings & his thoughts into words.
He is working in Odia film industry as an actor, story writer and assistant director.
His Instagram handle is @coolcapt_abhilash.
He has taken part in more than 75 anthologies.

Road Of Life

Life is like that road which,
has too much twist and turns.
In life you always know,
where you need to reach,
But sometimes it is difficult,
to depict the path,
you need to follow.
Just carry on your life,
the way you want it to be,
time will guide you,
In your journey of life.
if the road is unknown to us,
we need a guide to,
reach the destination,
in the same way if the,
path is unknown to the,
zenith then time acts as a guide."

Precious Life

Value every moment of,
your precious life.
You never know what may,
happen just in the next moment.
It can be that the next moment,
is as happy as you have,
Znever faced such happiness.
Or the next moment can be,
as sad as news that you have,
never thought of it in your dreams.
You never know when, and,
in which way your life can,
take a twist and turn.
It all depends upon the Almighty,
how he would like us,
to lead our life."   ""

Lessons Of Life

Live your life the way you want,
don't be under any pressure,
specially the pressure of,
this society and friends.
Only you and your parents have the,
right on your life as,
they are the ones who have,
given birth to you.
Your parents are your well wishers,
never leave them for,
someone else who is mean.
You never know in which,
turning of your life you,
will need the support of your parents."

Asmita Bansod

Asmita is a 19 years Veterinary student. She's passionate about writing and has co-authored many books. She's also fond of singing and songwriting

Getting Dressed: A Beautiful Experience

Getting dressed seems such a huge thing. It's harder than solving a physics or maths problem for me. It's so much work. Plus it consumes a hell lot of time. Getting dressed in today's world is not just putting that outfit thing on you. It's much more. As far as my knowledge goes, which doesn't goes far enough, getting dressed is an attempt of being someone else, so that you look worthy of people's praises. Dressing up can have ample of meanings, right from putting on clothes to decorating things in an artistic way. It's up to you what you want it to mean.

I remember the the first time I got dressed. It was for a farewell party. My entire family was so excited for getting me dressed that the preparations began a month before the actual day. It seemed like a wedding preparation. Everyone in my family was a part of that 'getting HER dressed thing', except me cause I hate getting dressed in their ways. It's really hard when you are the most favourite and loved one among your cousins. You are so loved that getting you dressed for your farewell party becomes their lives primary mission. As expected it was long journey of selection of the DRESS and entire stuff going along with it. I'm estimating a minimum of ₹10K wastage, just for 3 hours of celebration.

The big day arrived. I wrapped myself with the DRESS. After that there was a 2 hours long session of painting my face. Then I wore my jewellery and 5 inches high heels and looked in the mirror. I was shocked. I asked, "" Is it really me?"". Yeah, I looked beautiful but fake. When my parents looked at me they were surprised. I took a step ahead and as expected I fell down. I was a 15 years old teenager who couldn't walk in heels. All they wanted from me was to look like a girl and carry myself with utmost elegance and grace. Well I failed. I ruined the crease of the DRESS and then my heels broke because of my excessive weight. In a moment I was again a clumsy girl. A girl who likes wearing simple and plain clothes. It was not acceptable, a normal teen girl is not supposed to dress like an Amish woman.

Then I stole a glance of me in the mirror and I realised getting dressed for people's praises is not my thing. Painting my face, wearing a satin laced dress is not necessary to be a beautiful young lady. Walking down and carrying yourself with confidence and grace is necessary though. I got up, cleaned my face, wore one of my plain lavender coloured dress , applied a little bit of lip gloss, fit my feet in a normal sandals, and as for cherry on top of the cake, I wore my mom's vintage earings. Then when I looked in the mirror, I saw myself. I confidently said ""Yes, it's me"". Simple, elegant and beautiful. Your attire does not define you. Although your attire must go along with the occasion.

Well one thing I learned that day was , I am better off with my sweats. I don't have to wear a pretty dress and paint my face to prove that I'm a beautiful young lady. I am who, who I am. I accept and love myself. I don't care what people say cause I am comfortable in that loose T-shirt and those baggy pants. I experience happiness in that. All those people who say I won't ever be able to make a man fall for me because of my dressing style, well I just want to say I don't want to be with a man who judges me by my dressing style. I'm not against getting dressed, once in a while for special occasions is mandatory. When it becomes an everyday task it's just peer pressure. Dress for yourself. Dress for embracing the joy of getting dressed. Being yourself is more important than looking beautiful. Beauty which we all apply is fake and fades away. Just start beautifying your heart, start dressing your hearts. My heart is beautifully dressed. And your's?

Reshma Bhattacharyya

Reshma Bhattacharyya is a simple housewife from small town Giridih, Jharkhand, India. Originally she hails from West Bengal, India. She did her Bachelors and Masters both in English Literature from University of Burdwan, West Bengal, India. She loves travelling a lot and exploring new things. Teaching is also one of her passions. Writing poems, short stories blogs and expressing her thoughts is her favourite passion. It soothes and calms her mind. She loves it doing very much and tries her best to express the exact feelings to reach reader's mind and touch their feelings.

The Teacher In Me

Many a times, some incidents happened with me,
That which I hadn't planned but it came by chance,
The experiences which I gathered, made me more matured today.

Just like a moth, hovers around the flame of a candle,
I was wondering for a perfect goal to be successful.
When again by sheer chance, I chose to be in a very novel profession.

A profession of teacher, where one gets respect, dignity and self-confidence.
While as a teacher, I can't express the love and respect which I got,
Yes, then I realised teaching is my forte.

Being a teacher, I felt myself satisfied,
To impart good values and principles,
My heartiest gratitude to all teachers
Who devote themselves solely for the welfare of the students.

Quote

My life's journey has taught me a very crucial lesson that nothing in this world is more valuable than loving and respecting oneself

Aysha Afrin K M

She is an English Literature graduate, who currently is a teacher in training. She started working straight after graduation abroad for a year then quit to pursue higher education and to actually do what she likes to. Her greatest dream and passion is to become a published author and she is slowly taking those small steps towards the heights she has set. She started writing when she was 14 and has continued it over the years. Besides writing her interests include cooking, reading and she in love with music, western especially. She hopes to become a writer and a best English teacher in her future. Let's hope she gets it.

To The Beautiful You

I guess with age comes the most clear visions. I was always afraid of getting abandoned. Until I left everything. I discovered a relief in that. And I guess at one point in life, each of us would that. Just to keep ourselves sane, running away, hiding, and finding excuses. And now understanding why everybody do that, it doesn't even make me angry anymore, it doesn't, ""

Life is bitter. There are times you have thought about leaving everything behind and run away. To you, at that particular point of time, this would be the only solution, everything you have in front that hinders you. Some do dare to do, while most of us decide not to, thinking of the co nsequences of leaving the comfort zone even when you're tired of it. But it's not because you hate people, it's not because you're tired of the family around you. It is because you're momentarily tired, temporarily in need of a change and need to taste something new. But many around us do not understand until they are under pressure and decide to do the same, and have the same level of thoughts and packages we just went through.

This is life. Nothing more, nothing less There will always be ups and downs , there will always be lots of losing and winning, there will always be anger and tears, but we are not the bad guys. We are not cowards. We are brave but just a little tired. We are courageous to make decisions but back out thinking about the people we are responsible and care for, we choose ways not just for us, we choose for those we see as priorities, and if the world fails to see that goodness in us, it is never our mistake. It's naturally theirs. And we will always be victorious, at one point we will be also happy.

She Belongs.

“Come in” her boss called her in. “Sir I guess this is the work for today. I have completed everything, I need your approval.”

“Feature as come out well, keep up with your work, you might get promoted. Sub-Editor isn’t a bad post at all for you.” He said.

“Thank you sir” her heart fluttered listening to the comments he made, her dreams coming true. Her hard work finally going to be paid off.

“Sir” she turned back to him. “ Is it okay if I leave early today?” she asked for his permission to return home early.

She wanted to celebrate the news with her husband. Her boss knows well how the newly Weds are these days. He smiled and let her off.
She took her bag, corrected her suit and rushed out of the office. ‘He would reach by 8, so I should prepare the dinner by 7.30 at least to surprise him. God life is so refreshing. I can’t imagine declining the job I have got now. London has been in my dreams for a really long time. I have finally achieved it.’ She thought smiling widely as she stood in the line for billing in the super market.

She prepared his favorite dishes getting instructions from her mother in law. She put on the black dress he bought her the last week. The deep V neck was showing off her cleavage but she liked it. She put on the pumps and looked at herself in the mirror. ‘Perfect dress for a date night’ she thought unable to stop smiling. She seemed to be leading a very happy and successful life. She applied some make up and went downstairs to see him coming in after work. She worried if he would be tired. But to her surprise she saw him coming with a boquet of roses. She opened the doors for him. Love was in the air around them. He changed to some comfortable clothes and began to help her set the table in their backyard. She told him about her upcoming promotion. And they sat for the dinner. She was happy as ever. But she was shy to still look into his face being married only for few weeks. Her heart pounded louder every time she caught him staring at her. She blushed. The rain began to pour down. As she began to clean the table, he stops her and gives her a back hug pulling her closer. He turned her and kissed her gently on her lips for a long time while she tried hard to catch up with her breath. She was melting. The rain poured down on them but it did not stop them. He took her in his arms and walked inside the house. She was exactly where she belonged wrapped up in her happy place, in her happy land.

She suddenly woke up from her dream, it was dawn, she looked around her dark room. The bed was empty.. He seemed to have spent another night away. She struggled to get up with the saree wrapped tight around her hips. She was sad. She wasn't allowed to ask where he was and what he was doing. Mother in law doesn't seem to like questioning men in the house. She showered and changed to another saree.

A frame fell down from the wardrobe while she arranged the clothes. The photo of hers with her friends on her graduation day. The frame shattered into pieces. She cut her fingers while she picked up the broken pieces of glasses, tears falling down her face. She took the photo out of the frame and placed it between her copy of "Gone with the Wind" novel. She was sore still in pain even after two days spending the nights with her husband, unwillingly without consent and in rejection. Her chances turned into painful dreams killing her everyday. But those words echoed in her head “be a good wife”. She cried and cried while she pretended to be a happy bride.

Abirami B V

Abirami B V did her M.Phil Research in English Literature at Annamalai University. She did her master's at Pondicherry University. Currently she is residing in Neyveli, Tamil Nadu.

Two Sides

Darkness ends
Brightness begins!
Sorrow ends
Happiness begins!
Doubtful ends
Cheers start!
Lie ends
Truth sprouts!
Hopeless ends
Trust begins!
Fear ends
Peace begins!
Hatred ends and
Love begins!

Uncertainty

Don't believe!

Life will be same as you think. Everything will change, don't know what happen next.

Woman

A woman is a human
Where, she get many names from this society.
When she is alone, she tries to console herself.
People mock at her.
Sometimes she frustrated.
Sometimes she never mind.
She accepts all, but not all time!

Love

she waits for him.
He too waits for her.
They both waiting!
They have hope, and the days are passing like clouds.
Each day their mind wandering each other.
Their memories begin to act and their emotions overflow.
They express in different ways.
She cries all night.
She wants those nights, where she spent with him all alone!

Dr Sayanee Saha

Dr. Sayanee Saha is a gynaecologist by profession, who belongs from Jalpaiguri, WB~ a proud daughter of Mr. Uttam kr. Saha and Mrs. Rubi Saha, who have been absolutely amazing parents to her in this beautiful journey of life. Although a surgeon by profession, and a writer hidden to her core, she has been scribbling down since her childhood, but took up writing as an excelled hobby amongst others only after realising that it has been a hidden passion dug deep somewhere with a brisk twinkle, awaiting for the spark to ignite it into sheer illuminance.

Writing to her is like thoughts skating into a multifaceted cube of myriad emotions and curating a beauty through etched words.

She wishes to be able to sway your hearts by creating poetries that you may find either sumptuously relatable or drenched in vivid imaginations.

To know more about her, you may follow her work under the Instagram handle @the_ornated_quill

She

The scarlet petals that glittered her evasive lips in sunshine,
Those clandestine curves in her which you considered divine.
The untouched dew on those sharp edged grass blades,
Those epiphanic moments to cherish before it slowly fades.
The melancholic tunes of your old rusted guitar,
That urge to walk maybe a little further.
The slaughtered purples of sky in a beachy sunset,
And the silent altruistic prayers before you go to bed.

The moistened kohl of sleepless nights,
The uncut silence of tireless fights.
The lost fragrance of those dried lavenders,
The barren conflict you never meant to surrender.
The sharp pricks of fervent winter rains,
The brisant music on repeat that drives you insane.
The abhored emotions that were never at ease,
The galloping heartbeats you vehemently tried to appease.
She was much more than what you had known of her.

Behind the storms of silence,
Breaking the shackles of destiny,
Beneath the clouds of misery,
'She' walked with her head held high, leaving for you a mystery,
you could never decipher in binary!"

ज़िन्दगी की रहगुज़र"

कंधो से ज़मीन और ज़मीन से कंधो तक का सफर,
चार कदमो में तय ये ज़िन्दगी की रहगुज़र!
दिल को चुभता आज भी तुम्हारे शब्दों का ज़ेहर,
जैसे वक़्त के दो पल में गया हो ठहर।

उस सफर का वाबस्ता थोड़ा सा सुकून अब चुन लो,
मुस्कुराके यादों की मोतियां तुम बुन लो,
आयने ने भी तुम्हे यहाँ कैद किया नहीं,
तस्वीरो में छुपी हँसी की ठाँके खुद ही सुन लो।

वक़्त के रफ़्तार में खो मगर न देना तुम ये गुलाबी पहर,
चाहे फिज़ाओं से बाँट लो पुराने ख्वाबो का लेहर,
फरमाइशों की चिट्ठियां पहुँच जायेंगे तुम्हारे शेहर,
बस कंधो से ज़मीन और ज़मीन से कंधो तक में तय ये ज़िन्दगी का
सफर!

You Have A Fight Left In You

You thought that the colour palette of life was bleak,
The emotions cascading within you were sick,
A beautifully fading song lost somewhere in a wreak,
At a quandary to choose which path to pick.

Let me hold your right there,
Shake the vibes in you and tell you fair,
No prince to arrive out of nowhere,
So cut the false aspirations and beware!

The world may not hear your clamours,
Because knights don't always spring in shining armours,
Those shedding tears in inundating showers,
Amidst hopes of climbing the tallest towers,

You still have a fight left in you!!"

Gaayathri Maya

KK Gaayathri Maya is a final year student at Pondicherry Central University and currently taking up her second Master degree In Sociology. As a she is from both literature and Sociology field, her interest towards arts and societal activities are high towards both. Gaayathri is also passionate about dance, drawing and writing poems which completes and fulfills her. She is a well rounded individual who lives with passion nd grace.

(1)

The secret of happiness
Is When you stop searching it
Because when you wait for something
Or
When you badly want it to happen
That never happens
Why so? Even your hair doesn't grow when you want it too...
Lol!"

(2)

Some people are like assets
Some people are themselves lessons
Some more are like gift wrapped bullshit
Some rare ones are beautiful memories to be treasured
And
The choice is one's own
With whom our travel is going to be...

(3)

The world is not,
What you actually see
But
What you experience
It curses you at times
It showers love in times
Sometimes
It breaks you
Curshes you
But Still
At the end
How far you have been matters! "

Ruchi Vachhani

Ruchi Vachhani, born and brought up in Mumbai, presently in Nashik, Maharashtra. Working as an architect. Hobbies include painting, writing, reading, travelling, dance, photography. Have achieved 1st rank in traditional dance form, 1st rank in motion photgraphy and various certificates in art competitions. Outside work, is an outgoing person and helpful. Likes to explore new things and places around the world

The Journey :To A Better Tomorrow!

She knew she was different! She wished that her life would be exactly how she thought of! But that is what life is all about, right? The ups and downs, the sad and the happy, the lefts and the rights. We get what we least expect, we receive that we wish for, or let's say what we believe in. This time life gave her a second chance, to survive, to lead, to learn, to be happy, to achieve and most of all to believe in herself. Isha, a girl from a village-not so greatly populated, let's say some hundreds of people. She lived with her mother and her brother. Yes! She was the only daughter of her village, to survive. She was capable of doing things that any boy could do. But most of all she was the favourite and was loved by all! She was a fighter, a beautifully grown woman known! Isha was adopted by her mother! She was found fighting against the contagions faced by mostly girls from around. But she fought and came out strong. She proved to be a living example of strength, love, compassion, determination and discipline for a girl to be! She was a wonderful dancer, a disciplined student, a compassionate person towards her dreams and a determined daughter towards her responsibilities. Yes! Her dream was to help maximum of people from near and around and give them a better living. And she strived to work hard on those dreams. She adopted her career in teaching, not only in schools but also experimenting various things to make living easy and long termed. She lived by her laws, but at the same time, she was flexible enough when time required. Ten years and Isha is now one of the best-known lady experimentalists for improving living efficiency and providing a better living program for those who really needed to survive situations which are unimaginable. She took the chance life gave her, without wasting a minute on wondering what should be done next. Yes, she also got lost in her journey while running towards her dreams, she in fact also gave up many a times but she looked at herself, swept off all the stress, believed and started working towards her goals! But in this journey of hers she never concluded her tasks, she just went on doing it as days passed and eventually with lots of failures too, she succeeded in her works. With so much in her life to do, she was happy, because she knew she was the one to help herself out, she did because she believed in herself. She was and will always be an example for how to turn opportunities to gold, and still remain happy and grounded for the people. Her motive to help all the people out there, who are not even recognized was being achieved as she was on her journey. The journey to a better tomorrow! "

Daughter Of Universe!

Surprises! Right. Life always surprised her, but she never turned her back on them rather fought back with a smile. A girl with minimum needs, she still stood out among many due to her generous nature. Many judged her for who she never was, but only few knew the real her. Lucy, a girl from the city grew up with her mother. Excelling in all aspects of life she grew to be a strong and independent woman. She believed in praying to the universe and always thought herself to be a part of it. "Hey Lucy, how are you? How is life going o n?" people generally used to ask her. And she used to reply with the kindest of the words she could, smiling in every situation you could imagine. Lucy had a bad habit of laughing or smiling at serious times. But she controlled making it the most difficult task for her. Lucy, born with one of the rarest contagions, fought for her life when she was 7 days old. And guess what? She nailed it like a champion. Yes! she definitely was a warrior. She grew to be a happy child, playing, doing mischiefs and at the sa me time being a good girl and an excellent student. Let's say she was allrounder for a girl to be. Praises and appreciation were all she needed to reach her achievements. And she nailed it all again! But this time her role turned out to be of a fighter. Her life was perfect until she started understanding reality. Surprises! Remember. Lucy expected her life to continue the way it was since her childhood; she fantasized her favourite people to be immortalized so that they could be with her till her last bre ath. But life is all about letting go and acceptance. The sooner she understood it the better her life became. She believed that she was different than others around her. People said she had the purest of heart any person can have, even as a normal human b eing, she understood that love, kindness and courage is what it takes to reach the main goals of life. She had no grudges for the difficulties she had to face, she also did not complain but fought back with the same energy and attitude every single time. A nd that's what defined her to be a warrior, which gave her the courage to help others and be present for them when they most needed her and she nailed that too! And this time like the daughter of universe, as if she was born for this purpose, giving life a surprise by her strength and love."

Saheli Banerjee

Amateur writer and poet whose writing mainly follow the wordsworthian philosophy of ' spontenous overflow of Emotions'.

An english Major from West Bengal, and speciality in Greek Mythology, she is an educator by proffesion. Her book " Pools of Blood" is available in www.Dreame.com
And another book " Murder Of A King" is available at www.goodnovel.com
You can know more about her and her poems on her website www.gobuSpeaks.com/blog
Her Insta Id : saheli_gobu

Cries!

I stood in between
My ears splitting with the loud cries,
Of a joyful mother and a teary wife.

The death of a father of an unborn child,
And the melodious 'uludhwani' to welcome the bride.
I stood in between
Hearing both the tumultuous cries!

One son leaving his parents behind,
Another son is giving the cause to smile,
The child would never see his father again,
I stood watching both the scene
With tears of joy and pain!

This is the rule of the world of God
One goes away and another takes its pot.
Cries and smiles, tears and laughter
This is the mystery of the Nature!

I stood in between
The candles and lights brightening a home,
Another is plunged in darkness and gloom.
My house lies in between the two.
I stood watching both the views!

A Painful Night

I am weak...I am not strong
I'ven't done anyone wrong,
Why its me who suffers the most?
I am dead...I am lost.
I can remember the first time I cried,
How I wiped the tears,
Buried the pain inside..
All my memories good and bad that's passed
Didn't even take time to realise..
Staring at the crack in the wall,
Waiting for it all to come to an end,
Still I curl up right under the bed,
'Cause its taking place over my head,
All over again!
Lying awake..watching the sunlight..
How the birds will sing,
As I count the rings around my eyes,
Constantly pushing!

Shreyansh Shreshth

I'm a writer but not a professional.. Halling From Patna. Pursuing my BTech from N.I.T patna
Insta id- @kalam.kaar

Hug

There's something in a simple hug
That always warms the heart;
It welcomes us back home
And makes it easier to part
A hug's a way to share the joy
And sad times we go through,
Or just a way for friends to say
They like you 'cause you're you
Hugs are meant for anyone
For whom we really care,
From your grandma to your neighbor,
Or a cuddly teddy bear
A hug is an amazing thing -
It's just the perfect way
To show the love we're feeling
But can't find the words to say
It's funny how a little hug
Makes everyone feel good;
In every place and type,
It's always understood
And hugs don't need new equipment,
Special batteries or parts
Just open up your arms
And open up your hearts."

December night

Everytime I try to write about you
I end up sinking my own heart.
I try not to remember you anymore,
but every december
I end up bleeding my own heart.
Everyday I pretend that I've moved on,
but every december
I find myself on the same path.
The path which doesn't lead anywhere,
But there is no way to go back from here,
as the bridges to my heart
are all now broken and shattered.
I am stuck here without you
and the worst thing is
I still don't want you."

07:00 A.M

This short history
Of ours seemed
Like forever,
Didn't it—
I guess love can
Really stop time
If you let it, for me
It's still stuck at
7a.m and everyday
At that hour, I still
Hate looking at my
Notifications, I'm
Sure soon that hour,
Won't mean much.
But today, it still feels
Like the end of a sharp
Knife being stopped
By my very own heart."

Aditi Palmate

21 years old girl, currently in 3rd year MBBS at Mumbai. To epitomize, her life is all about Sketching faces, Reading minds & Healing people. Overthinking everything drives her insane. Weaving words keeps herself sane !

Change

Flaming summer will change into freezing winter.
Hectic Monday will change into serene Sunday.
Lazy morning will change into fascinating dawn.
Weeping night will change into fun night-out.
Ugly scar will change into brave memory.
Fierce fear will change into substantial power.
Scary silence will change into ceaseless chatter.
Miserable matter will change into huge hope.
Reckless behaviour will change into compassion.

Hey, don't be harsh on yourself..
This is meant to change.
Change is a challenge which cannot be resisted.
Change is the only constant!"

Amruta Makode

She is a soft skills trainer and an Academician hailing from city of lakes Bhopal. She is an enthusiasts in dancing, creative writing, story telling, anchoring and traveling. Her articles and stories have been published in news dailies, story books and magazines.

The Magical Pen

Being on stage, I could see some familiar and some unfamiliar faces. There is a story behind each and every face .As, I was getting down from the stage, just then a little girl approached me with a book in her hand and said, "Autograph please!"I took out my old Wilson silver colour fountain pen and signed on the front page of the book .Looking at that shining Wilson silver colour fountain pen, my mind went down the memory lane.

"Amruta, come fast sit behind my scooter we need to hurry up !",Baba (my dad)shouted .The Bajaj scooter's accelerator was on full race ,bus stop after bus stop and my daily chase of school bus began. I was supposed to board the bus at Tilak Nagar but as usual I had missed my school bus again. Riya (my elder sister) had already boarded the bus but I was left behind. To my astonishment that day was my Mathematics examination. Anyhow I had to reach school on time .I was the laziest out of the three siblings. I was in a school where there were strict rules and discipline. It was the last place I would ever want to visit, unfortunately I was supposed to go daily .The fear of attempting a Mathematics examination was giving me goose bumps. Distance=Speed x Time, Profit =Selling price – Cost Price. I was memorizing such formulas in my mind .Oh God !solving mathematical problems was definitely not my cup of tea .One night before the exam Riya had taught me short tricks and important questions .One of my biggest fears at that time was to attempt a paper of Mathematics. So we were chasing the bus and finally the bus stopped at the Mall Road. The bus driver was an elderly figure, with a white beard .As soon as I boarded the bus he started shouting at me, "This is your day to day habit, You are always late!" I boarded the bus anyway. I was sitting beside a window seat .Baba asked me, “Do you have a pen”? Before I could answer anything Baba gave his own sliver colour Wilson fountain pen to me through the window. In a hurry, I took the pen from him .Just then the bus started moving. After that I checked my pencil box and I was amazed to find out that I had forgotten to keep a pen. I was wondering whether it was a paternal instinct or a coincidence. I wrote my exam with that pen and cleared it.

Since that day this pen is with me in all ups and downs of life .I believe that it is a blessing from my father. During my journey of life from childhood till now, this pen has been my constant companion. I did not stand alone but what stood by me is unconditional love of my father , acting as a strong pillar of moral support. This unconditional love makes this pen priceless and magical.

“Wow! what a big day for all of us, Amruta, hurry up come for a group photograph”, Baba called out .I came back from flashback to present. I was still looking at that sliver colour Wilson fountain pain. Today was my first book launch event, a day to remember for sure. .Yes,it is the same magical pen using which I had given my first autograph ,today. That too on the book written by me .Then it was time for a happy group photograph which was also a memorable moment!

Dr. Rwitu Ghosh

Dentist by profession, heals tooth ache in her practice and tries to heal heart ache with her words.

Dare To Dream

Each time I was told I could fly
I would hurt myself willing to try
Each time I didn't qualify their yard sticks and tests,
They told I did not give my best.
These voices like noise;
Deafened me yelling,' You have no choice'
I was gasping and choking under their expectations and pride
For no one I loved was on my side
Then like a blessing few people came
Who helped me to change my plans and game
Through them I came across people like me
In despair, struggling or have given up on their dreams
These angels in disguise held my hand and said,' Don't worry, it's never too late,
We know you can make through that success gate,
We know its your lone fight
But we will stay by your side.'
Hope lit up again;
Neither the soul nor the body minds
To leave no stone unturned till happiness it finds
Now ,buckled up for new adventure, all the past roads I cease;
I am a wanderer now in search of peace
To all who told me,' When they can, why can't you? '
With a smile, I reply,' For I know, I am good at something that they cannot do.'
So this is my journey, my new-found trail;
Where eyes are full of dreams,
Where attempts can but the 'will' will never fail.

Unloving You From Now

Loving you is like loving a cactus
For I have the bruises of your affection all over me
Every morning you leave me faster than those marks on my body
I tried to convince myself that it was normal
While relentless tears streamed down my face
Did my love ever feel toxic?
Did you ever feel like my love was strangling your neck?
Did you ever feel you were drowning ?
Did you ever plot escape?
Then tell me why your love makes me feel so ,
Leaves me with a strange feeling that I dread but know
I was so broken once that I craved for love
So when you showered all your attention I fell for you
That manly grasp around my wrist and your tight hugs
Made me feel I was needed
But now it's somehow all different
I really feel angry at the sight of you
Hate the way you caress my hair and skin
I am tired of hiding the marks
For a long time , I thought
What we had behind those closed doors was just normal
But now it's time to close my door on you"

She Is Not Used To

She is not used to praise
Nor a pat on her shoulder
She is an average girl
Maybe invisible for her moderate caliber
Not a pretty face; so you can skip,
But if you talk to her, you shall see—
She dreams;
Though she's used to them not coming true
This fire and unfathomable belief she has in her
Might reignite your failed hopes too.
She is not used to love ;
But even the slightest care can melt her ,
And if you can match her vibes,
That's your ticket to her world—
Full of smiles and adventures,
Not even close to perfect;
She is a wild mess instead ,
But there is something in her eyes,deep like ocean ;
You'll surely be lost once you dive in ,
Like some enchanted music you long to listen
Her voice her stories are so alluring
She is there for you when you turn back
And also infront, like a shield ,protecting you from harm
She is there with all songs of praise
Encouraging you and cheering you with constant affirmation
She is a patient listener
A silent supporter
A reliable friend
But she is not used to praise
Nor used to too much love
She is easy to love;

much easier to unlove and let go
But if you know her ;
You'll realise she is not that easy to forget,
For when you got used to her you don't even know.

Diya Mehta

Diya Mehta now in her teens is a born writer and poet. She started writing poems from the first year she entered her teenage She is dedicated and enthusiastic towards her writings . She expresses her views and feelings in her poems well enough.She is also an artist by heart. Diya is from New Delhi and she is climbing the ladder of success by the support of her parents. She is a simple and sober girl trying to make a difference in the society.

ज़िंदगी

दो दिन की ज़िंदगी है यह ,
आज ख़ुशी कल ग़म ,
आज बचपन कल जवानी ,
आज जीवन काल मरण ,
जीलो इससे जी भरकर
वापस ना आएगी यह ज़िंदगी ,
जी हाँ बुलाने पर भी ना आएगी
जुगनू हो तो लेलो किसी तारे की चमक ,
खुद चमको और चमकाओ ,
यही है दो पल की ज़िंदगी
बढ़ेंगी मुश्किलें होंगी परीक्षाएँ ,
हार जीत ही ज़िंदगी है !
ज़िंदगी , चलना सिखाएगी , गिरना सिखाएगी ,
लेकिन गिरकर चलना ही ज़िंदगी है ,
इसलिए ज़ीलो यह ज़िंदगी ,
लव यू ज़िंदगी !"

ज़िंदगी का सच:

ज़िंदगी होती ह
उसने प्यार होता है
यारी दोस्ती होती है,
उसी ज़िंदगी में,
जोड़ने वाले बहुत है , तोड़ने वाले बहुत है ,
जनाब फ़र्क़ सिर्फ़ इतना सा है ,
कौन जोड़ रहा है और कौन तोड़ रहा है ,
जीलो ज़िंदगी के इन छोटे लम्हों को ,
क्या पता यह
आगे बने यादें या बने ख़ुशी के आँसू !
पल भर का है यह जीवन का फूल ,
इससे आँसू दोगे तो मुरझाएगा ,
ख़ुशी दोगे तो खिलेगा ,
यादें दोगे तो हँसेगा ,
ग़म दोगे तो रोएगा ,
इसलिए ज़िंदगी के फूल को खिलने दो और खुश रहो !!

दिल और ज़िंदगी

यह ज़िंदगी की कहानी है ,
यह बहता हुआ पानी है ,
इसके पत्थर , पीतल आएँगे ,
लहरे आएँगी , तूफ़ान आएगा ।
जनाब
रूकावटें बहुत है लेकिन बढ़ाने वाले सिर्फ़ आपके दिल में है ,
तूफ़ान में तो घने काले बादल भी आएँगे,
उस अंधेरी रात में रोशनी सिर्फ़ आप ही बड़ाएगे ,
विश्वास रखो अपनो पर ,
दूसरे आएँगे और जाएगे ,
ना करने वाले बहुत है ,
पर कराने वाले गिनती के ।
आने दो रोशनी सूरज की ,
अंधेरा होने दो अंधेरे में ,
प्यार करो अपने आप से ,
और विश्वास रखो अपनी मेहनत पे ,
बार बार न खुलेगी ज़िंदगी की यह किताब ।।"

Avnish Kumar

अवनीश कुमार हिमाचल प्रदेश के बिलासपुर जिले के रहने वाले 22 साल के युवा हैं , वह अभी Master's in Animal Science की पढ़ाई कर रहे हैं, उन्हें शायरी ,कविताओं से बड़ा लगाव है उनका मानना है कि जो जज्बात आप किसीको बताने से डरते हैं या छुपाते हैं शायरी उन्हें ब्यां करने का एक दिलचस्प ढंग है।

Insta I'd - avnish_d_himan

खुद की ख़ुशी :

आसमां के नीचे एक नए मकान की छत पर अकेला बैठा हूं तन्हा हूं,
कोई भी नहीं यहां जो मेरी एक बात तक सुनने को तैयार हो,
हजारों ख्याल दौड़ रहे हैं मेरे दिल में कचोट रहें हैं मुझे,
हां मैं दुखी हूं कोई भी नहीं जो इस दिल का हाल समझने को बेकरार हो,
हर शख़्स मज़ाक बनाता है मेरा पागल समझता है मुझे,
शायद कोई भी नहीं जो इस दिल का सच्चा यार हो,
इस दुनिया के सितम सहने की शक्ति अब बाकी नहीं बची मुझमें,
अब फ़र्क नहीं पड़ता चाहे जैसा भी खंजर इस दिल के आर पार हो,
मेरा बस नहीं चलता मेरी खुद की मुहब्बत पर मैं बेबस हूं उसके सामने,
मैं तो उसके जिस्म पर भी हक नहीं चाहता बस दुआ है मेरा इश्क़ पाक़सार हो,
जिसको भी अपना मानता हूं किसी के पास वक्त नहीं है मेरे लिए,
अब कोई भी नहीं जिसे मुझे अपना कहने का अधिकार हो,
दिल कहता है कूद जाऊं इस छत से इस कहानी को खत्म कर दूं,
आख़िर कोई भी ऐसी बात नहीं मुझमें जो मुझे खुद से प्यार हो,
कोई इच्छा बाकी नहीं है इस दिल में गर मर भी जाऊं तो गम नहीं,
लेकिन मैं नहीं चाहता कोई भी मेरी वजह से टूट कर तार तार हो,
जिंदगी का एक एहसास ये भी है जो रोकता है मुझे खुद की ख़ुशी से,
कहीं यूं ना हो मैं चला जाऊं और किसी की आंखों को जिंदगी भर मेरा इंतज़ार हो,
ख्याल मेरे असल अपनों का आता मुझे जिनके रुख पर नूर है मेरे होने से,
फिर क्यों गैरों की वजह से मेरी खुद की बनाई हुई ये हस्ती बेजार हो।

वक्त :

जिंदगी के मुश्किल वक्त में, मैं उससे उसके वक्त की उम्मीद कैसे रखूं,
जब इस खाली वक्त में भी उसके पास वक्त नहीं है मेरे लिए।

उधार :

एक अरसा हो गया था हमें जिंदगी से खुशियों की उधारी मांगते मांगते ,
आधी उम्र गुजरी तो एहसास हुआ कि आखिर ये जिंदगी खुद ही एक उधार है ।"

Shilpa Sahu

She loves to express her feeling , thought and observations through writting

सफर

मैं अपने सफ़र में कई बार भटकी हूँ,
चलते चलते बेवजह सी बातों पर अटकी हूँ..

जिस राह भी चलती हूं
,सही लगने लगती है,
पर कुछ दूर जाकर मैं फिऱ पलटने लगती हूं..

मेहनत नहीं ,पर कहीं मन लगाना असल खेल है,
जो मन ना टिके कहीं, तो सारी मेहनत फेल है..

निराशा की आँधी ने कई बार मुझको तोड़ा है,
तिनके भर की आस से, मैनें हर बार खुदको जोड़ा है..

मेरी नाकाम कोशिशों का सिलसिला अभी जारी है,
क्योंकि सकारात्मकता से मेरी घनिष्ठ यारी है..

हाँ मैं हारी हज़ार बार हूँ ,एक जीत की तलाश में,
पर जो हार मान लूँ कभी तो समझना एक लाश मैं !

जिद

वो सपना नहीं ख्वाब हैं

वो ख्वाइश नहीं जिद हैं

नजाने कितने अरसे से उसे सिचा हैं

कितनी रातो ने उसे बुनते देखा हैं

आसुओ के बाड में भी वो बाहा नहीं

घुसे की आग में भी वो जला नहीं

कई लोगो ने कोशिश की उसे मिटने की

पर वो कम्बख्त मिटा ही नहीं

भुला केसे देते उसे वो सिर्फ सपना नहीं

ख्वाब हे जो हकीकत होने वाला हैं

कुछ अरसे बाद पूरा होने वाला हैं

वो ख्वाब पहचान बनाने वाल हैं

वो ख्वाइश नहीं जिद हैं

जो पूरा होने वाला हैं

दर्द

मै बतलाती नहीं पर दर्द होता है मुझे भी,

लगता है सबको की कठोर हु मै,

पर क्या करू आँखो मे आंसू बतलाती नहीं मै किसी को,

लगता है सबको की समझती नहीं मै,
पर समझ कर भी नासमझ बनना आसान है,

आदत नहीं है मुझे अपने आंसू दिखाने की,

पर इससे मै कठोर तो नहीं,
आंसूओ को छुपाना आता है मुझे, पसंद नहीं,

रोती हु मै भी पर आंसू किसी को बतलाती नहीं,

पर इससे मै कठोर तो नहीं,

दिल है मेरा भी जो कभी पिघलता भी है,
पर फिर भी मै बतलाती नहीं,
जतलाती नहीं की दर्द मुझे भी है,

पर इससे मै कठोर तो नहीं,

अक्सर आँखो मे कचरा चला जाता है,

जब भी किसी को आंसू मेरा कोई दिख जाता है,

पर इससे मै कठोर तो नहीं,
दुख है मुझे भी, दर्द मुझे भी है,
दास्तां मेरी भी है कुछ,
बस मै बतलाती नहीं,
छुपाती हु मै आसुओ को दिल मे अपने

पर इससे मै कठोर तो नहीं !!

Saira Siddiqui

"Saira Siddiqui, is an epigrammatist. At present she is working as a lecturer in Hyderabad. Apart from teaching, she enjoys trying new recipes.
She believes that, "Through the writing one can express the unknown facts."
On the advice of her best friend she started writing and since 2019, she is been expressing herself through her quotes & poems.

Her works can be read on: www.yourquote.in/sairasiddiqui"

Unapologetic Life

Start the journey of life

then make youself realize

when you freez the past

then you can do the blast

life is given to celebrate

time has come to accelerate

not to demote but to promote,

panic may stop you to float.

have a grip over the mind

put the doubts in the mixer & grind

not everyone is meant to be there in life

their leaving is a lesson to imbibe.

be your own inspiration & identify

the life is to be led by & not to say good bye

Medicine Of Life

To brighten up your life
I've advise for the naive
Take it everyday like a pill
Then only you   can stand still
Swallow, to sharpen your brain
Then remove the dust of pain
I'm sure you'll feel better."

Chaotic Life

Life is not at ease
So as mood
Mind is not at peace
So as actions
Heart is not healed
So as relations
Eyes are empty
So as emotions
Now everything is upside
down as you are not
around."

Sanchana Jayakumar

Sanchana Jayakumar lives in Chennai. She is a software developer by profession and she has always been passionate to write and her love to write is just to share her thoughts to others.She is a budding writer and hoping to learn and explore a lot as a writer in future.

Bucket List One!

The day has come where she was all set to start her trip with a lot of unknown people having connected with just one of her colleagues. Yea, the trip that most girls would have one in their bucket list to travel around and explore. It would not have been a dream come true moment without that office mate who joined Sanchu with her friends to the trip. It was an all-girls trip. With so much of emotions, excitements, thrill and many more happenings to Sanchu throughout the trip that gave her lessons, confidence, strength and will power to face any challenge she had to face going forward in her life. Sanchu was basically a too sensitive in nature and was not always independent in her daily life. Sanchu had to take her first trekking on the very first day of the trip and it was a three km into the forest area with just two guides with them and all girls. Sanchu was scared but she gave her best to continue the trekking without disturbing anyone else and slowly moving to see the beautiful sunrise at the other end of their trekking end point. With so many hurdles, fear and even hesitation to have opted for the trekking, she finally got to view the amazing sunrise that vanished away all her negative vibes that she had during the trek time to reach the hill top. Sanchu was now stronger and grew confident to give her maximum efforts to return back to the tent stay and then again, she had to face hurts but never bothered and continued to give a bang with all the support she got from her office mate and her friends. Then when all were about to reach the tent stay again they had one big rock to pass through and Sanchu was scared to do it as it was her first attempt to do rope trekking and she burst into tears as she failed to do after so many attempts .Then,Sanchu was very much morally supported and encouraged by all around there and finally with the help of one of the guides she could finally reach the tent stay. She had a great sigh and that incident was a lifetime experience that she could never forget as it made Sanchu both emotionally and physically stronger than before. Sanchu had started her bucket list and she was determined to enjoy her life to the maximum of she can as it is just her theories and learning and experience, she get in each walk of her life. Sanchu is really blessed to have Latha the one behind all the initiatives for her achieve her one of the dreams to be true. Sanchu accepted the fact that we do meet people for a reason and some become very special and important as days pass on, one such person was Latha to Sanchu.

LIVE
LOVE
TRAVEL

An Inpirational Love

She is an inspirational person to many people around her and a love for me. She was born in a family where she was celebrated by all as she was a single girl child with so many brothers and relations to be protected and nurtured still in a strict way to maintain the dignity of her family and make her a bold and strong woman in this world. She was married at the early age of 21 to a person whose family had so many people to be taken care of and a good lot of responsibilities. She had a challenging life style from then and even now though she is surrounded by some good ones to be taken care of her. She was an extra ordinary and excelling student in her studies and she was so motivational and pushed herself to bring up her little family to a good state and with all hard work being paid of after ages that was still a good sign for the rest of her life. She was about in the process of bringing up so may small children with good confidence and guidance to whatever field they are in after years of her experience in her profession. Yes, she is a TEACHER. She was so respectful and lovable to those little ones for almost 30+ years in her field. She is none other than my own MOM. It is such a blessing to have been her daughter and getting to know her story from a simple human to becoming a more of an inspirational women that makes me boost myself when I fall every time in my life. She is the best gift of my life. Thank you, Mom, for all you have been to me and You always be my Inspirational love.

Khanida Firdose M

Khanida Firdose M is 21 year old student from Bangalore City. She is pursuing MA in Literature from Bangalore City University. She loves to read novels,write thoughts, blogs and stories. She aspires to become a renowned author in future. As well, her another goal is to become a College Lecturer so that she can transform the lives of the students. She is a co-author of anthology - " Diary of Emotions " and "Miniature World of Minds" and is also a co-author of other anthologies which are soon going to be published. You can read her blogs in WordPress (firdosekhan.wordpress.com) You can also explore her writings in her instagram handle : @writings_firab

Sophia

Divya has trust in me. She knows that I will secure more than 90percent. But I am puzzled because my maths paper wasn't good as other subjects. I told divya to check my result. She clicked the submit button and the result appeared. Divya hugged me with the tears rolling down. She was so happy that she could not control her tears.

Congratulations Sophia. You have secured 92percent, she said. I wasn't able to beleive her words. I saw the screen to make sure of her statement. And it was true. I was speechless for a moment. And then I hugged Divya. Thank you so much Divya. This could not have been possible without your support and love , I remarked.

No it's not me who's responsible for this, it's your hard work and sacrifice which made it possible. As well , it's the support of your parents. First go and thank them instead of thanking me, she insisted.

Though they are not my real parents, they have given me more than enough. God has blessed me with the treasure for which I longed to have. I was born in a remote village of Andhra Pradesh. My parents are illiterate and my father is a drunkard. Beyond this, I belong to an impoverished family.

My dad believes that a girl is born to serve the men. As well he thinks that education spoils the mindset of a person. So he never sent me to high school. He let me study till 7th standard because of my mom's pressure. After my 7th standard, he forced me to go and work in my neighbour's house.

Fortunately, Ridhima aunty decided to send me to school instead of making me work in their house. She had told my dad that I am working in their house but instead she would let me attend the classes. Every evening after my school, I would help her a little bit. From then till now, I wish Ridhima aunty and Rohan uncle were my real parents. They have given me so much without expecting returns from me.They don't have their own child yet they loved me as if I am their child.

I reached home. I saw that Ridhima aunty was praying in the prayer hall. As I entered, she embraced me. I know you have secured good percentage Sophia. You don't have to tell me because I always knew that you will make me proud one day, she exclaimed. Yes aunty I will never let you down, I assured.

Ridhima aunty had prepared my favourite food items. I devoured the delicious food. In a flash, I saw my father entering the house. He seemed to be very furious. He came in and banged me hard with his belt. Ridhima aunty tried to stop him but he pushed her away. He held my hand tightly and forcibly carried me along with him. I was continously lamenting but he didn't care. I understood that he might have known the truth that I was studying instead of working. I left the place helplessly.

According to the recent research, latest data puts India's adult literacy rate at 73.2 percent. Even though the country has made significant progress in improving literacy rate, it continues to be the home to 313 million illiterate people; 59 percent of them are women.

Every Indian has to be aware of this data because only when a person is aware about the facts he will be able to spread awareness. It's not only about Sophia , it's about so many other children who are forced to work instead of studying. We being a responsible citizens, have to create awareness and contribute to the needy as much as possible. I beleive that ""Maturity comes when you stop making excuses and start making changes"".

Master Piyush Kranti

"Master Piyush Kranti, a person with a smile as big as his name.
Can be seen either trolling his haters or putting his earphones on to detach from rest of the world. His sarcasm never goes out of trend.
Thinks that writing down is the best way to present onself.
This believer of Karma, is currently in the first year of his grad school
Apart from an amateur writer, he's a big foodie and loves to explore cusines all over the world. Family and friends are his source of support and inspiration.
He's a 'Any problem!? I'm just
a call away...' type guy."

The Unsipped Cup Of Coffee

You remind me of a warm cup of coffee.

The soothe you bring in with every sip of your love makes me crave more of it.

It's been a while since I touched you with my lips.

The warmth of your aura and the late winter's chill, make me long for your presence around me.

You left me like we had nothing between us and this winter has made all of those shattered emotions come back.

Hope you read this someday and realise what you meant to me.

Till my last breath,
~Your Departed Love.
"

Note To The Society.

I fear darkness, for the gloom it brings
I fear to love, for betrayal it is awarded with.
I fear to express, for the fact that my voice shrinks
I fear to smile, for the tears it hides beneath.

I want to fly high, so high that the birds envy
But then the fear of everything pulls me down
I could see the society look at me with a frown
Burning my wings of desire with their jealousy,
They kill the voice inside me,
They bury me in the soil so deep that I can hardly see a light.
But they forgot that I was a seed,
Meant to tear the breast of the Earth,
I rise, I grow, I spread and I prosper."

Her Wingless Flight.

She was a bird,
Meant to fly high.
And that's why the society wry.
They tried to cut her wings,
Make her suffer from worse things.
But she was a fighter,
She held her sword tighter
She fought the world bravely,
And that's why she's loved and respected greatly."

Saloni Lal Srivastava

She is Saloni Lal Srivastava daughter of Mr. Kumar Prashant and Mrs. Asha Sinha from Siwan, Bihar. She is a girl from a small town with her big dreams. Her life is all around her family, friends and career. In present she is purchasing B.sc in Botany hounors. She work as co author in 25+ anthologies. She is one of those who love to spread smile and positivity to everyone. Her instagram handle is @salonilalsrivastava.

दोस्ती

यह एक ऐसा अल्फाज है जिसको सुनते ही सुकून मिलता है। एक सच्चा और अच्छा दोस्त किसी की जिंदगी में ठीक वैसा ही होता है जैसे अंधेरे में जलता हुआ दीया। लेकिन हम यह भी जानते हैं कि किसी भी सिक्के के दो पहलू होते हैं। अगर कोई सच्चा दोस्त किसी की अंधेरी जिंदगी में जलते दिए कि समान होता है ठीक वैसे ही एक बुरा दोस्त किसी की जगमगाते जिंदगी में अंधेरा ला देता है। यह खून का रिश्ता नहीं होता खून के रिश्ते से ज्यादा हमारे लिए जरूरी हो जाता है।हम आपने सारे राज तक उससे बांटते हैं। वह भी अपने दिल की हर बार बिना कोई हिचकिचाहट की हमारे सामने रख देता है। एक ऐसा ही सच्चा और प्यारा सा दोस्त मेरी जिंदगी में आया तो था और एक बहती हवा की समान चला भी गया। बिना कसमे वादे की शुरू हुई यह दोस्ती हम दोनों की जिंदगी में जैसे खुशियों की सौगात लेकर आई। लेकिन कहते हैं ना हर कहानी का खुशियों भरा अंत नहीं होता। ठीक वैसे ही हमारी दोस्ती का भी अंत हो गया पर किसी फिल्मी बॉलीवुड की कहानी की तरह खुशियों भरा अंत नहीं हुआ। वह तो एक असल जिंदगी सच्ची दुख भरा,समझौते से भरा एक दुखी अंत था। हम दोनों एक दूसरे से बिल्कुल अलग होते हुए भी एक जैसे ही थे।ना कोई जलन, ना कोई प्रतिस्पर्धा बस एक बहती नदी के समान गतिशील थे। मैं उसे एक पिंजड़े में कैद रखना चाहती थी ताकि कोई उस तक ना पहुंच सके, उसको किसी की नजर ना लग सके बस मेरा ही दोस्त बन कर रहे। लेकिन वह एक आजाद ख्यालों वाला हमेशा आसमान में बिना कोई डर के उड़ना चाहता था। उसको दुनिया देखना पसंद था और मुझे उसे दुनिया से छुपा के रखना। धीरे धीरे वह मेरे विचारों में ढलने तो लगा था लेकिन वह कहते हैं ना यह ज्यादा दिनों तक नहीं हो पाया कुछ दिनों बाद उसे फिर से उड़ने की इच्छा होने लगी। मुझसे दूर होने लगा। तब जाकर

मुझे भी समझ आया कि हम किसी को बांधकर नहीं रख सकते।अगर हम, किसी से प्यार करते हैं, किसी को अपना मानते हैं तो उसे एक आजाद पंछी की तरह खुले आसमान में छोड़ दे अगर वह हमारा होगा तो कहीं नहीं जाएगा वह लौटकर खुद हमारे पास ही आएगा। कुछ दिनों तक सब ठीक चला। जैसे हमने सपने देखे थे सब कुछ धीरे धीरे जैसे हकीकत बन रहा हो.. हमारी खुशी का कोई ठिकाना न था। पर शायद हमारी खुशी को किसी की नजर लग गई थी। पता नहीं अचानक उसे क्या हुआ वह कहीं दूर चला गया, हमारे सपने फिर अधूरे रह गए पर मुझे अपनी दोस्ती पर पूरा विश्वास है सुबह का भूला शाम को घर जरूर लौटकर आएगा और फिर हम लोग अपने अधूरे सपनों को पूरा करेंगे। फिर होगी भविष्य में हमारी यह प्यारी सी कहानी पूरी बॉलीवुड स्टाइल में पूरी। और मुझे यह पूरी उम्मीद है कि हमारी कहानी का भी खुशियों भरा होगा तब तक मैं इस कहानी का अंत नहीं होने देना चाहती।बस हमारी जिंदगी एक शांत और सुकून भरी रास्ते पर एक दूसरे के साथ चलती रहे। जैसे कि कोई मंजिल ही ना हो और कभी रास्ते खत्म ही ना हो बस प्यार से हमें एक दूसरे के साथ चलते ही रहे।" ....

Ashish Kumar Singh

Ashish lives in Prayagraj, Uttar Pradesh. He has completed his post graduation from BHU, Varanasi. He loves to write on emotions what an individual feels. He writes on happiness, love, expectations, hope etc. He believes in Karma. He always inspires others to do better in their life and to be happy
Add my Instagram id: @anjaana_raahi

जिंदगी के लिए जीना जरुरी है

जिन्दगी के लिए जीना जरुरी है,
दूर होते हुए भी पास दिखना जरूरी है।
हर वक्त तो ना हो पायेगा एक जैसा,
मुश्किल वक्त में भी मुस्कुराना जरुरी है।

वक़्त के कई मोड़ आएंगे,
कभी खुशियां तो कभी ग़म लाएंगे।
वक़्त के हर मोड़ पर संभलना जरुरी है,
जिन्दगी के लिए जीना जरुरी है।

तुम कभी रोशनी सा मुस्कुराओगे,
तो कभी घने अंधेरे में छुप जाओगे।
उन अंधेरों में भी चमकना जरूरी है,
जिन्दगी के लिए जीना जरुरी है।

तुम कभी रास्ते में लड़खड़ाओगे,
तो कभी खुद से गिर जाओगे।
लड़खड़ाते हुए खड़े होना जरूरी है,
जिंदगी के लिए जीना जरुरी है।

सपने कभी धुंधले से दिखेंगे,
तो कभी ख्वाब टूटते से लगेंगे।
उन ख़्वाबों को बनाए रखना जरूरी है,
जिन्दगी के लिए जीना जरुरी है।

सुन प्रिये !

मैं खुली किताब सा, तू रखे सारे राज प्रिये !
मैं नदी की शान्त लहर, तू भूलभूलैया घाट प्रिये !

मैं सुबह की धूप सा, तू सयानी रात प्रिये !
मैं उछलता सपनों सा, तू खुद पे रखे नाज प्रिये !

मैं सपनों का राही, तू हकीकत में साथ प्रिये !
मैं बातों का सौदागर, तू खुद में ही जज़्बात प्रिये !

मैं मंदिर का शंखनाद, तू आरती का आगाज़ प्रिये !
मैं संध्या की गंगा आरती, तू घंटी की मधुर आवाज़ प्रिये !

मैं पतझड़ के बिखरे पत्तों सा, तू फूलों की मुस्कान प्रिये !
मैं अमावस की अंधेरी रात, तू खुद में उजला चांद प्रिये !

मैं राह में बिछड़ा हुआ काफिर, तू मंजिल की शान प्रिये !
मैं आंखों में खोई उम्मीद सा, तू चाहत से अंजान प्रिये

इश्क और प्यार

तू परवाह दिखा, हक नहीं
तू सवाल कर, शक नहीं।

तू पास रह, दूर नहीं
तू प्यार कर, फितूर नहीं।

तू मुझे समझ, लोग नहीं
तू मरहम बन, रोग नहीं ।

तू एहसास कर, जुनून नहीं
तू दर्द हर, सुकुन नहीं ।

तू जिन्दगी बन, ख्वाब नहीं
तू इश्क कर, हिसाब नहीं ।

तू खुशियां बटोर, फिकर नहीं
तू आंखों से पढ़, जिकर नहीं।।
"

उम्मीद

जिंदगी है तो चलना भी जरूरी है,
घर से बाहर रहना, आदत नहीं मजबूरी है।

कौन चाहता है अपनों से दूर रहना,
पर अपनों के लिए जिन्दगी जीना जरुरी है।।

दुनिया की इस भीड़ में दिखना भी जरूरी है,
आगे बढ़ते हुए रुकना भी जरूरी है।

हर वक्त ना बन पायेगा एक जैसा,
सपने देखते हुए थकना भी जरूरी है।।

माना कि जिन्दगी में संघर्ष बहुत है,
पर उनसे डट के लड़ना भी तो जरूरी है।

ये आसमां यूं ही तो हासिल ना होगा,
उसके लिए जमीं से उठना जरूरी है।।

Hermit

an impatient immortal soul bloomed within a fragile pollen driven by a flux of perspective chimeras

My Pet Demon

When the red sun hid behind the grey curtain
And the vagabond breeze rushed in,
I was roaming inside the purple forest
Looking for the magic mushrooms.
As I hovered briskly over the dead leaves
From between the spooky bushes
Heard a footstep loud and strange.
In fright, my owl eyes explored around.
But before I took the next breath
An envelope of darkness filled my eyes,
And at once I fell down asleep.

An odour so sharp crawled in through
My nostrils, and woke me up from my sleep.
As I woke up, I saw a giant ghoul
Walking out from the shadows.
With frightening red eyes, stained pointy teeth,
And an axe in his hand dripping blood everywhere
He looked like the demon prince of hell.
Where have I dragged myself in this time?
I wondered.

I tried telling myself that there is nothing to worry
And all of this is nothing but a nightmare,
But the rusty hefty chain that held me strapped
To the wrecked tall walls of the chamber,
And the ponderous shrieks of the demon's footsteps
That came closer to me, told me otherwise.
Mustering all my strength I turned to him and asked,
Who are you? Why am I here?

"I am the protector of balance,
Warden of virtue;
He who has strayed from the path of truth
Ends up in my dungeon.
Here you begin your new life, the righteous life,
Offering me your present life, the sinful life."
Words are fucking time machines;
And the ghoul's words reminded her.

Those nights that I moaned of bad days,
My mother used to tell me that
It is the demons that check upon us
And not the gods, in the afterlife
There will be no heaven to resurrect to
But only the hell to pay for our sins.
Every moment that we are alive
We are in heaven and only a fool
Will make both his life hell.

The ghoul dragged me by my hair
To a room with a huge and tall closet.
Two of its columns covered
With hanging silver threads,
But the middle one kept open
As if he was about to put something in.
And in the faint light, I realized
What he was going to keep in it.

Like mementoes, he collected and preserved
Countless severed human heads,
From which the green blood of their souls
Dripped down drop by drop,
On to the ledger of their sins.

And whilst sharpening the edges of his axe
He looked at me and said,

"Your body is a vessel
And you have polluted it.
Today I will free your rotting soul
From this corrupted skin,
And tomorrow I will resurrect you again
In a different skin,
This is your day of salvation.
This is your day of redemption
I am your savior."

The gleam of the blade sent a scare,
To parts in me, I never knew existed.
Crouching down I blurt right out,
I know I've sinned, and I beg
That you let me live to right all my wrongs.
But so swiftly came his axe;
An icy nick along my neck,
It should have set my head rolling on the floor,
It should have been my end.
But slowly my eyes opened
And there I was, in the forest,
A half-eaten mushroom in hand,
The fruit of the conquest I set out on!

Moitry Das

An amateur litterateur trying to find her calling in this complex world. Infatuated to solitude yet rebellious at heart. Finds solace in poetry and music. Excited by the rain and coffee.

Reminiscence

Incandescent bulbs and coffee beans.
A soft white pillow on the other side of a teardrop.
The cool zephyr brings in the fresh petrichor,
A heady concoction of memories and heartbreaks.
Of wars and death.
Of newly mowed lawns and returning home.
A mother's sob and a grandmother's hope.
It's strange.
What a few drops of nostalgia does.
Fills the crevices of the mind with the sweet syrup of ecstasy
while agony too joins the party.
The raindrops follow a disciplined parade,
Each walking towards gravity like a soldier.
Like a son returning to his mother.

Yash raj

yash raj is student by profession ,writer as hobby and passion, he is person who loves to write poetry and quotes,who likes eating, gyming and capturing every moments of life. he is gym lover. Honesty,truth and loyalty are the main mantras of him life .

IG : @toxic_dark_world

तु कोशिश कर सब हो जाएगा।।

तु कोशिश तो कर सब हो जाएगा
जिंदगी के इस सफर में नौका लिए एक दिन तु भी समुंद्र पार जाएगा
इस भीड़ भरी दुनिया में एक दिन तु भी अपनी पहचान बनाएगा
देर लगेगी पर तु कोशिश कर सब हो जाएगा

हार कर रुकना मत थक जाए तो कुछ पल ठहर कर फिर शुरू
करना जो तेरा है वो तुझे जरूर मिल जाएगा
तु कोशिश तो कर सब हो जाएगा

कभी खुद पर शक होने लगे या हारने के डर से कदम पीछे हटने
लगे तो देखना अपने मां बाप की तरफ एक कोशिश फिर से उनके
लिए करने की ठान लेना तेरा सपना जरूर पुरा हो जाएगा
तु कोशिश तो कर सब हो जाएगा

जो सपना देखा उसे पूरा करने की शक्ति भगवान देगा
और सपना पुरा ना हो तो निराश मत होना
क्युकी कहते है ना।। मन का हो तो अच्छा ना हो तो और भी अच्छा
क्युकी वो भगवान की मर्जी है

तो बस भगवान की मर्जी समझ कर एक बार वापस आगे बढ़ जाना
तेरा भी दिन आएगा
तु कोशिश तो कर सब हो जाएगा
तु कोशिश तो कर सब हो जाएगा"   "

जन्म

जिंदगी का सफर कुछ यूं शुरू हुआ,
आज एक परिवार में उस बच्चे का जन्म हुआ।।

परिवार में खुशी ,जुबान पर उसी बच्चे का नाम है,
हाथो में मिठाई है और बच्चे आने की खुशी अपरम्पार है।।

दादा-दादी मां-बाप बुआ-फूफा चाचा-चाची हर कोई उससे मिलने के लिए बेकरार है,
यही तो परिवार हे जंहा एक फूल के खिलने से सभी के चेहरे पर मुस्कान है।

घर में बेटे का बेटा,दादा-दादी के आंखो का तारा,चाचा-चाची का दुलारा,बुआ-फूफा का प्यारा भतीजा आया है,
देखो तो सही एक परिवार में खुशी लिए हजार खुदा का एक अनमोल तोहफा आया है।।

उस बच्चे का जन्म जो हुआ,
उसकी जिंदगी का सफर अब शुरू हुआ,
उसी के साथ सभी की जिंदगी में नए सूरज का उदय हुआ,

ये सभी जिंदगी के अनमोल एहसास है
दूसरों कि खुशी में सब खुश है
यही तो अपनों के लिए अपनों का प्यार है।।।

एक सवाल

जिंदगी एक एहसास है,
कुछ खट्टा कुछ मीठा सा इसका अंदाज़ है,

जिंदगी तुझसे एक सवाल है,
ये सब तकलीफ तेरी मेरे ही साथ है,
या अभी यहां सभी का यही हाल है,

कभी फूलों की तरह खिल जाती है,
कभी लापरवाह होकर इस आसमान कि सेर कर आती है,
कभी परवाह के बीच फस कर एक कमरे में समेट जाती हैं,

कभी दूसरों कि खुशी के खातिर कुछ भी कर जाती है,
कभी दूसरों कि खुशी में जल भुन भी जाती है,

वाह रे जिंदगी तेरा भी क्या एहसास है,
कुछ खट्टा सा कुछ मीठा सा तेरा अंदाज़ है,

बड़ा खामोशी का दौर है अभी
जिंदगी थम सी गई है
खोने को कुछ हे ही नहीं
क्युकी कोरॉना के इस दौर में कुछ बचा ही नहीं

लोग परेशान है
हर इंसान हैरान है
इस दौर का होगा कैसे अंत
सभी का बस यही सवाल है।।

Suman

She is a tender executive. She is from delhi. She likes to write and whatever she feels.. She is loving by nature.

God You Are Here:-

God you are here??
God I don't believe that you are here.
If yoy are here, why didn't you come to wipe the tears when I kept you calling..
God I have lost my close one, I prayed for him,
Why didn't you accept it???

God you are here???
Why didn't you come to me??
Why didn't you ask me about sadness..???

God you are here??
Why I am always being cheated???
If I am good with everyone..

God, you are here???
Why I was got alone??
Why I am feeling to suicide...???

God if you are here?? Full filled this wish..
God, I don't want anything in life except my family.. Please give them happiness.."

जिंदगी ने मुझे बहुत कुछ सिखाया:-

जिंदगी ने मुझे बहुत कुछ सिखाया ।।।
समझता था मैं लोगो को अपने जैसा पर क्या पता था कुछ लोगो का दिल होता है सैतानो जैस।।।

जिन्दगी ने मुझे बहुत कुछ सिखया।।।
खुशी में सब शामिल होंगे तेरे
दुःख में तू अकेला होगा।।

जिन्दगी ने मुझे बहुत कुछ सिखया।।।
अच्छे लोग होते है बहुत कम।।
बुरे लोग होते है बहुत ज्यादा

जिन्दगी ने मुझे बहुत कुछ सिखाया ।।।
तु सिख ले अपने ज़िन्दगी जीना क्या पता कल तू हो या न हो, तू सब से तो लड़ लेगा लेकिन तू भगवान से कैसा लडेगा।

जिन्दगी ने मुझे बहुत कुछ सिखाया ।।।

I Want To Be Butterfly :-

I want to be butterfly
Because I would be the reason of Peace and light in someone's life...

I want to be butterfly
Because , with the colored wings I spread my beauty for each and all to see.

I want to be butterfly
When I get sad , I would spread my colorful wings in the sky...
I want to be butterfly I would fly fearlessly , where I wish I would fly.."

Shubham Raj

Shubham raj is student by profession,writer as passion.He loves to portrait feelings by his words in poetry and quotes.He enjoy moments of life. He is a nature lover.

Insta id : @Shubhamraj2784

जिंदगी

हर रोज की भागदौड़ मे खोती जिंदगी
ऑफिस की फाइलों में गुम होती जिंदगी
याद आती है वो बचपन का तराना
बचपन की वो खुशियाँ , वो अपना यराना
ना दिल मे कोई बैर था ना थी नफरत किसी से
ना धर्म , ना जाति, ना थी द्वेश किसी से
उम्र थी कच्ची मगर ना थी शिकायतें किसी से ।

ना जाने जिंदगी क्यों अब बदली सी लगती है
जवानी भी अब हमें धोखे सी लगती है
अब हम बड़े हो चुके है इसांनियत से दूर हो चुके है
वो बचपन की मासुमियत शायद बचपन में ही भुल चुके है
छल कपट से भर गयी है अब जिंदगी
खुद को ही खुद से दूर कर गयी है ये जिंदगी ।

जब बचपन में थे तो बड़ा होने की होड़ थी
अब बड़े हुए तो जिंदगी ही एक दौड़ बन गयी
शायद तब जिम्मेदारियों का बोझ ना था
खुशियाँ थी होठों पर, आँसुओं का एक कतरा भी ना था
गलियों मे था वो बचपन अपना
अब तो घर के आँगन मे भी जगह ना थी ।

अब मुश्किलें तो आयेंगी हर एक मोड़ पर
इन मुश्किलों में रोने से अच्छा है,
चलो खुशियाँ तलाशते है
जिंदगी से शिकायतें तो बहुत है,
चलो जिंदगी जीने की वजह तलाशते है

खुद पे भरोसा कर चलो इसांन बनाते है
चलो एक बार फिर से जिंदगी को जिंदादिली सिखाते है ।

एहसास

उस पल का एहसास जब माँ पहली बार आपने छुआ था
उस पल का एहसास जब पहली बार मैने माँ बोला था
उस पल का एहसास जब पापा ने चलना सिखाया था
उस पल का एहसास जब आपने मुझे गोद में सुलाया था ।

कैसे भुल सकता हुँ वो एहसास
जब पहला अक्षर लिखना था आपने सिखाया
नींद ना आने पर लोरी था आपने गाया
थोड़ी सी चोट लगने पर पुरा घर था आपने सर पर उठाया
पापा से डाँट पड़ने पर अपने पल्लू में था आपने छिपाया ।

हाँ, कैसे भुल सकता हुँ मैं वो एहसास
जब खुद भुखा रहकर आपने मुझको था खिलाया
बाहर पढ़ने जाने पर पापा से ज्यादा पैसा आपने दिलाया
मेरे फिक्र में अपना शरीर था आपने गलाया
जरा सा परेशान होने पर मेरे सर को था आपने सहलाया ।

कैसे भुल सकता हुँ माँ वो एहसास
जब मेरे सलामती के लिये हर दर पर आपने सर था झुकाया
मेरे भविष्य के सफलता का रास्ता भी आपने ही बनाया
हर छोटी-बड़ी गलतियों को माफ करना भी आपने सिखाया
भगवान ने भी बड़ा तरासकर था आपको बनाया ।

हँ, वो माँ का रुप ही हो तुम जिसने इस संसार को चलना सिखाया
कैसे भुल सकता हुँ वो हर एहसास जो आपने महसुस कराया
माँ वो एहसास हो तुम जिसको पाकर हमने जन्नत को पाया ।

पीरियड्स

हम जो इसपे बात करने से इतना शरमाते है
बता दू तुम्हें बाप हम इसी क्रिया से बन पाते है
हम आधुनिक युग में जी रहे है
लेकिन whisper आज भी काली पैकेट में खरीद रहे है
क्यूँ इन्हें सबसे अलग कर दिया जाता है
दर्द भी चुपचाप ही सहना सिखाया जाता है
किसी को पता ना चले घर में भी यही बताया जाता है
जब कोई पुछता है पूजा क्यूँ नहीं की
तो सर झुकाकर उसे समझाना पड़ता है
जब बाँधी थी राखी रक्षा की
तो फिर क्यूँ नहीं उसे भी यह समझाया जाता है
दर्द में भली रोती रहुँ, पर पापा के सामने मुस्कुराना पड़ता है ।।

ऐसा लगता है जैसे कोई निचोड़ लेता है,पुरे बदन को जैसे कोई तोड़ देता है
खुन की एक-एक रिसती बुँद से तड़पती है वो
बिस्तर पर लेटकर सिसकती है वो
उन्हें हमसे कोई शिकायत नहीं है
जब तड़पे दर्द से वो, बस अपनापन का एहसास चाहती है
गर्म पानी की सेक से तुम उसके पेट को सहला देना
जब लगे उसे खाने की तलब तो प्यार से उसके लिए पका देना
पैड खत्म हो जाये उसकी तो बिना पुछे ही तुम ला देना
बालों में तेल लगाकर उसके दर्द को तुम मिटा देना
जरा सा प्यार देकर तुम अपना मर्दानगी धर्म निभा देना
पीरियड्स ही है कोई पाप नहीं बस ये कहकर
उसके सारे उलझनो को तुम मिटा देना
लड़की है वो बस उसकी अहमीयत का एहसास उसे करा देना ।

दुरियाँ

ये दुरियाँ खुद ही एक कहानी है
दर्द से भरी जरूर होती है
लेकिन जिंदगी में सीखा बहुत कुछ जाती है
पहली बार वो बचपन की दुरियाँ
जब हमें ज्ञान दिलाने को परिवार ने दुर किया
भले माँ रातों में रोती थी छुपकर
पर आँसुओं से कभी हमें ना रूकने दिया ।

वो दुरियाँ ही थी
जब माँ ने अपने बेटी को विदाई दिया था
भले थे आँसु आँखो में पर कभी हमें ना रूकने दिया था
वो दुरियाँ ही थी
जब एक पिता परिवार से दुर हुआ था
दर्द थी उनके सीने में भी, पर भुख ने उन्हें ना रूकने दिया था ।

हाँ, वो दुरियाँ ही थी
जब एक बेटे को अपने परिवार से दुर किया था
भले अरमान थे दिलों में बहुत, पर जिम्मेदारियों ने कभी ना रूकने दिया था ।
वो दुरियाँ ही थी
जब एक लैला-मजनु को दुर होना पड़ा था
प्यार थी उनके दिलों में भी बहुत, पर मजबुरियों ने उन्हें ना मिलने दिया था ।

वो दुरियाँ ही थी
जब परिवार को भी खोना पड़ा था
भले रिश्ते थे गहरे बहुत, पर मौत ने उन्हें ना रूकने दिया था ।

हाँ, वो दुरियाँ ही थी
जब एक माँ को बेटे से अलग होना पड़ा था
भले खोख से उसने जन्म दिया, पर कड़वाहटो ने उसको भी दुर किया था ।
हाँ शायद ये दुरियाँ ही है, जिसने मेरी जिंदगी को भी मौन किया था ।

Dr.Binayak Bibek Das

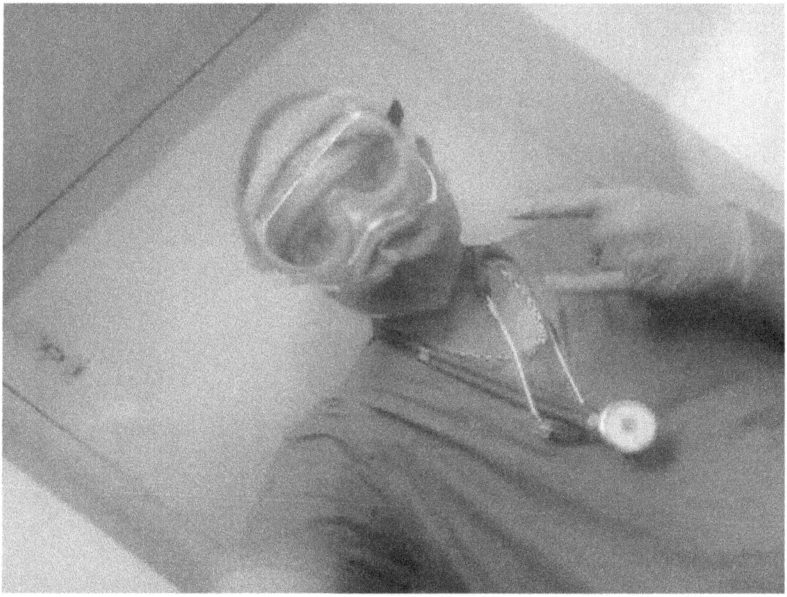

Dr.BINAYAK BIBEK DAS is a Eye surgeon by profession. He is a multi dimensional doctor who is good at all works.He is a master of almost all arts .He loves sports,travelling, photography,modelling and what not.Never ever quit and Uniqueness are his Life motto

ज़िन्दगी

ज़िन्दगी एक एहसास
ज़िन्दगी एक सास
ज़िन्दगी एक साज़

कब आए कब जाए
हवा के झोके के तरह
ले चले अपने साथ परिंदे के तरह

मैने बड़ी जददो जेहत से डॉक्टर बना
उसने मेरा हर गाड़ी इम्तिहान लिया
मैने भी हार नहीं मानी
और गगन चुम्बी चक्का
लगाकर इतिहास बनया
आज मैं एम एस ओफ्थल्मोलोजिस्ट रेजिडेंट हूँ
अपने सब बैच मेटस और दुश्मनो से बहुत आगे हूँ"

Alok Abhishek

Alok Abhishek, He is a ex banker having work experience of more than 2.5yrs with ICICI Bank Ltd. His hobby is to write poetry, mobile photography , reading novels and writing short stories. He is upgrading his skill in digital marketing area with the help of Shaw academy.

दिल

दर्द हो या ख़ुशी सब सह लेता है,
है कितना नादान छुप के कोने में रोता है,
अपनों की बातों को याद कर लेता है,
है कितना नादान दर्द में भी हस लेता है,
किसी ने तोड़ा तो किसी ने जोड़ा,
सब ने अपने मर्ज़ी से इस दिल से नाता जोड़ा,
कोई गम दे गया कोई खुशी,
फिर भी दिल हस के सब सह गया,
किसी के प्यार में धड़कना भूल गया,
वह छोड़ के क्या गया जीना ही भूल गया,
बेजान बेबस सा था , ना जाने कब पत्थर का हो गया,
पत्थर के दिल को धड़कना सीखा दिया ,
किसी अपने ने मुझे जीना सिखा दिया।
किसी अपने ने मुझे जीना सिखा दिया।।

पत्नी

रिश्ता यह बेहत ख़ास होता है,
जीवन का आधा सारांस होता है,
हर सुख-दुख में साथ होता है,
अमृत घोल दे जीवन मैं ,
यह रिश्ता इतना ख़ास होता है,
छोटे झगड़ो में प्यार छुपा होता है,
बात न ही तोह दिल बेचैन होता है,
तभी तो यह रिश्ता इतना ख़ास होता है,
कदमों की आहट को भी पकड़ लेता है,
दिल से जुड़ा रिश्ता बिन बोले सबकुछ समझ लेता है,
दिल से जुड़ा रिश्ता बिन बोले सबकुछ समझ लेता है,

रिश्तों

किसी के झूठ ने ज़िन्दगी भर का गम दिया,
किस्से करें बया ऐसा दर्द दिया,
झूठ को सच बना दिया,
कहना कुछ था, लेकिन बयां कुछ और किया,
भला इससे मैं अपनाओ कैसे,
दोहरे रिश्ते निभाउ कैसे,
एक बार खो कर जीना सीखा,
उस रास्ते को दुबारा न देखा,
समझाया था दिल को लाख ,
पर येह नादान,
न जाने क्यों तुझको याद करता है,
खुद तोह धरकता है,
आँखो को रुलाता है,
उन उलझे रिश्तों को याद करता है,
खुद तोह धड़कता हैं ,
आंखो को रूतला है ।।

Mitali Madhusmita Das

By profession she is an engineer,but for her passion is the key to win.she is always an optimist in worst.she is a learner and explore herself to get something new to pen down into her dairy.she always believes" life isn't complete until you feel the spirit of fearlessness because the spirit of adventure is in blood of one's".she is always in your deep thought to leave her experience footprints.she says dont share pain its worthless just ink it down in a dairy to make worth

My Experience Of Being A Woman

My daughter engaged today,
Her curiosity to know my experience,
Being a woman is justified.

Wearing a red saree ,bindis and bangles,
I came to house of my in-laws.
New rituals, culture,people and place,
Fear of handling situation,
Make upto their satisfaction supressed my dreams,
My partner became my courage to grow.

After years a baby born.
Yes,I became a mother in form of women,
Both complement and supplement to,
Realized existence of woman
In completion of man.
Man and women two wheels of carriage,
Neither can be what is in him or her to be.

Ancient scriptures assigned ,
power of woman ,
Represented the constructive aspects,
That blessed was the home,
Where I belong.

Traditionally the keeper of the home,
Managed the up-keep f house.
Bore children and brought them up,
Being the first teacher ,
Became motivation of my child.
Values and custom adopted by child,

In the lap of mother,
Being a mother in a woman is unparalleled.

Extreme sense of sacrifice and selflessness,
In modern india ,
Became a active patner in building of nation.
Handling arised problem,
Sacrified anger ,move forward without stop towards my passion ,
Which left behind my back.

To achieve my dream ,
Being exhibited women in form of mother.
Used leasure to my writting ,
Expressed my pain into pen down.
To earn self respect ,
From being a girl to,
Being a woman is development of personality.

Now my daughter is ready to stepped,
Into a new phase,
A brand new beginning of journey to experience in life,
Instead of dowry she took,
Courage and experience of mine,
To be an optimist in every phase .

Pratibha Kumari

Pratibha is a writer by passion as well as profession. She is too engrossed in reading books. She embraces solitude more often.

Instagram handle @ optimist_pratiba

Life Is An Experience

Life is about filling up the hollowness,
That has been created out of loneliness,
With the help of memories created on a convocation day,
Of the graduation caps flying high,
And the tears melting away,
Like the snow flake one at a time.
Life is like eating an ice-cream,
The more you procrastinate,
The more it is likely to drain away from you,
Take the first bite,
Even if you turn cold,
You will be able to judge its flavor.
Stop and observe,
Don't cry over the commodity you sacrificed to gain a new experience,
Smile, the experience will be buried at your grave
While the commodity will be transferred to someone else.

Himmat Singh Johal

He is a writer, a poet and a medical student. Inspired by his own thoughts and 'zindagi ke ehsaas'

A Helping Hand

* यहाँ जमीन भी है आकाश भी है, सब खुश हैं
कोई हताश भी है, हर चीज ज़ाहिर है फिर भी,
खुद को खुद ही की तलाश भी है।

One of my best life experience is that people will support you when you are down, they will help you lift up, that's beautiful. BUT when you start rising up, rise up and reach to there status they get jelous, you rise more and above them then the phase come when the person who was helping you yesterday starts pulling your leg today.
These people don't really help you they just do it for there publicity of being good. A helping hand is not always a helping hand, so be careful which hand you hold.

जिदंगी

* मेरी जिंदगी के कुछ अहसास ऐसे हैं,
कुछ जहर से कडवे हैं, कुछ मिठास जैसे हैं,
यहाँ लोग पल-पल बदल जाते हैं बदलते हुए
लिबास जैसे हैं|

* My soul is on fire,
But I'm not dead yet.
I have gone through hell,
But I'm not at hell yet.

Zindgi runs like a game, A level bit harder than the previous level, we pass one, another approaches with more difficulties but more fun and excitement.

The best teacher for one is your own 'zindgi ke ehsaas'. What you are is because of what you go through, what you will be is what you think right now.

औकात

There are a lot of words which defines you like status, reputation, class etc. But one word in hindi which have no specific translation in English is AUKAAT. The words defines you in this society, this single word limits you to the world. To stand out in crowd you need to beat this 6 letter word. If you beat this word, limitations end for you, you are a free bird now. So decide what your aukaat today is and your next goal is to beat that word. Set a mark and beat it, define your limits and break them.

Limitations are limited but sucess is not, your aukaat is a radius of your resources to utilise them but you can expand it by your dedication. "

(4)

People are important in life, all kind of. You like them or not, but all are important.

I have experienced myself running for a person of my intrest and leaving those who liked me, ended up loosing both.

In my experience the worst thing for me is dependence on others, I'm very uncomfortable to depend on others.

When you like or you hate a person, either times you are talking about thoughts of that person. So if his/her thought change, your intrest should change accordingly.

Talking about emotions I'll say it is the most beautiful but the most dangerous as well. It creates the worst fight ever in one's life, the fight between your brain and your heart. All you need is to balance your life on these two pillars.

Richa Tirthani

"She is a person who always believes in magic dragon and penning down people into the paper. So no wonder writing is her favorite.
She is daughter of Sunil Tirthani and Aarti Tirthani and moreover she love living life at her fullest
You can know more about her in her social media that is Instagram @richatirthani_05"

Life: A Story Of Dreams.

From the second you enter this universe,
Some days are meant to be beautiful and somedays curse.

In the path meant for you life pushes you along,
But never loose hopes because more than your difficulties you are strong.

Life is a roller-coaster ride,
Enjoy it fullest before comes the death guide.

Search for rays of happiness rather than crying,
Even if you can't still keep on trying.

The day you understand the subtle motive of your soul,
You will cherish your day and would get away from trolls.

Life is a small word but have thousands of emotion,
Sometimes fairy tale and sometime hell a dilemma of notion.

Life is like a fun fair enjoy its every bit,
Because the grasses are greener where you water it.

Keep on wondering and aiming for great things,
Because life is short and it can change in a single blink

Definitely we all have different plans along the way,
Daily we all learn something new and find out reasons to stay.

Our destination is a place far greater than we know,
For some this journey is quick for some its slow.

And when the journey finally ends we claim a great reward,
We either get onto hell or the house of lord.

That day u would loose everything u had once,
That time your wish to go along the luxury will not have even a single chance.

Sooner your body will decompose and would be left alone,
Before this nightmare make your life a beautiful boon."

Mihir Raghuwanshi

"Mihir Raghuwanshi is a student by profession. A writer and blogger by hobby. Addicted to fitness and sports.
He is worshipper of Indian Army."

ख्वाब एक एहसास

यह ख्वाब भी बड़े अजीब आते है, पर दिल को छूकर चले जाते है।।
कभी हमें रुलाते है तो कभी हासाते है, पर दिल को छूकर चले जाते है ।।
यह ख्वाब भी हमको वहीं दिखाते है, जिसे हम सबसे ज़्यादा चाहते है, पर वो दिल को छूकर चले जाते है।।
कभी ख्वाब होते है पूरे , कभी टूट भी जाते है, कभी मुस्कुराहटों का सवेरा कभी गम की शाम लेकर आते है।।
पर कुछ भी कहो यह ख्वाब दिल को छूकर चले जाते है।।"

Jyoti Duggal

Jyoti Duggal hails from Haridwar, Uttarakhand. She has completed her post-graduation in M. Com. and currently pursuing double master's in PGDBA. She is an educationist by
profession and a writer by passion. Her hobbies include dancing,
reading books, travelling and cooking. Connect with Jyoti via
–
Instagram: @jyotid19
Facebook: /Jyoti Duggal
E-Mail: jyotid1923@gmail.com"

In The Memories Of My Great Grandma...

So, it is my journey with my great grandma. the way she always makes me happy, motivated and energize my spirit to do more in my life. She always been an inspiration to me and there for me in my highs and lows..

I always remember the day when I was preparing for my 10th exams and got stuck with the thoughts that was bothering me throughout, she always motivated me to take 1step Closer to my success as she know that I am that capable to step out to my comfort zone but need some guidance n motivation from the one I love alot... She was always there to believe me that I can conquer the world as she saw some potential in me...

And, when my 10th exam results are out and she was the only one who was so happy and proud on me from that day she was always being there on my side. she always used to fight for me to pursue anything I want rather it is of the diploma course or to pursue my CS or to reach the highest peak on my dreams...

I remember the day when I Had a fight with my parents regarding my studies as they want me to pursue MBA but I always wanted to do something out of the box which my family never thought about. I have always wanted to do CS as my profession but due to to my great grandma's health issue I never thought to go far from her..

I know she can't stay with me forever but I never want to lose her last moments by staying away from her.. When she was in the hospital she woke up by seeing my face and had her meal by my hands only. She always used to behave like a kid when she was with me. We used to play games write Ludo late night and she told me all the experiences and the incident she have in her own life span of 96 years..

On her last moments too she used to call me just to sit with her and talk to her about anythingas I know she was afraid to loose me too. She was the one who made me a person what I am today and I owe my life to her. I always remember her lessons in my mind. I know she is not there with me now but I want to tell her that she is always there for me in my heart, in my life and nobody can replace her I miss you my Sherlock Holmes...

Vivek Maurya

He is student by profession ,writer as hobby. He is hobby person who loves to travel and playing games. He is tea lover. Honesty and truth are the main mantras of his life .
Follow him @_meri.jaan"

मेरी जिंदगी

हाँ........!

मै खुल कर जीना चाहता हूँ

क्यूंकि मेरी कुछ अधूरी ख्वाहिसे हैं,

वो मुझे ठीक से मरने नहीं देगीं,

लो पुरानीं यादें जो मेरी जीवन से जुडी़ है।

वो पल जो अब कभी लौट के नहीं आने वाले,

वो प्यार जो कभी मलहम बना करता था।।....

वो खिलौने जो कभी अब लौट कर नहीं आने वाले ,

पैसे नहीं थे पर चेहरे पे मुस्कुराहटें थी ।

बास आसमान में उड़ान की तैयारी के साथ ,

एक दिन चाँद पे जकर घुमने, खेलने की जिद।

वो ज्ञान - विज्ञान से प्यार ,अपनें सपनों से लगाव

सब ठीक - ठाक ही चल रहा था कि अजीब सा कुछ होता है।।

जैसे एक तूफ़ान सा आया और सब बदल गया !

वो सारे सपनों के बदल को कहीं और उदा ले गया।

जीनके बिन मेरा सपनो का आसमान अधूरा था।

बस अब उन सपनो को भुलाने की तयारी सुरु हुई।

जिसके लिए कभी मैं लड़ता
रहता था हर किसी से,

बस वो कहने को इक मात्र काश होके रह गया।

साथ ही सारी यादें वही दफ़न हो गयी।

मेरी पुरानी जिंदगी वहीं खत्म हो गई।"

Srishti Upneja

She is a student in profession with an intense desire to over achieve, a writer and blogger in hobby. She loves to write poem, shayari and quotes, and her contents are as wide and interesting as reality. She is an ambivert, and learns from every experience of her life.

Every glimpse of her has a secret that is expressed in what she write, which allows her to share best of herself.

खाली जेब

जीने के असल मायने
ज़िन्दगी की ठोकरें कराती हैं,
अंधेरे रास्तों को रौशनी की ओर ले जाती है I

लोगों की भीड़ में,
अपना कहलाने वालों में,
सभी अपने परायों से वाकिफ़ कराती है I

किस राह पर मुड़ना है
और आगे कैसे बढ़ना है,
गरीबी सही रास्ता ढूंढ दिखाती है I

ना-उम्मीदी में भी उम्मीदों पर भरोसा बनाती है,
हारे हुए इन्सान को,
उठ लड़ने की हिम्मत दे जाती है I

चोरी के रुपयों से खरीदे पकवान,
और मेहनत की कमाई से बनाई रोटी में फर्क क्या है,
ज़िन्दगी हमें ये बतलाती है I
खाली जेब काफी कुछ सिखाती है...

मेरा क्या दोष..??

मैं एक चिड़िया हूँ,
जो आसमान में उड़ना चाहती थी।
ना जाने किस नफरत में, पर काट दिए गए मेरे
अपनी लालसा में, मेरी मासूमियत तक को मिटा दिया।
अभी तो सही से जीना सीखा भी नहीं था मैंने
पहले ही मेरे जन्म लेने पर
अफ़सोस करना सीखा दिया तुमने।
मैं एक सहमी लड़की हूँ,
जिसे शुरुआत से अपनी शर्म में ही रहना सिखाया गया है।
इन हैवानो के बीच रह कर भी
मुझे कुछ बोलने का हक नहीं दिया गया।
आखिर क्या ग़लती थी मेरी,
जो अपनी हैवानियत दिखाने के लिए मेरा इस्तेमाल हुआ।
क्या इस पहनावे का है दोष, या दोष है मेरा लड़की होना।
सवाल क्यों मुझ ही पर उठ रहे हैं फिर आज?
शायद तुम्हारी ग़लती की वजह फिर बताया मुझे गया है।
हवस तुम्हारी, हैवानियत तुम्हारी
फिर भी इल्ज़ाम मुझ ही पर क्यों?

दास्तान-ए- दिल

वाकिफ़ हैं तेरे जाने के बाद के अपने हालात से,
मुसलसल अब आगे रोना नहीं चाहते।

ज़िन्दगी के खूबसूरत लम्हें,
जो बिताए तेरे साथ थे,
वैसा वक्त अब साथ किसी के बिताना नहीं चाहते।

ईल्म है हमें तेरी सभी रुसवाईयों का,
अब किसी की बेरुखी का शिकार होना नहीं चाहते।
दिल की बात हम समझना नहीं चाहते।

अपनी टूटी उम्मीदों से सवर रहे हैं धीरे से,
उन पूराने ज़ख्मों को दोबारा हरा करना नहीं चाहते।

थक चुके हैं अपने इन सवालों से,
फिर अपने दिल और दिमाग से लड़ना नहीं चाहते।
इसीलिए दिल की बात हम समझना नहीं चाहते।

Beyond The Boundaries

The life is standing to make you swirl on its fingers,
And people here are so inconsolable replete with sham.
Beyond the boundaries, is a new world waiting
which holds no hate within itself.

Reaching the limit is not an end to story,
Breaking bars and flying limitless is what you deserve.
Beyond the boundaries, standing your honour
which you paved this path for.

all failures have a new way to fight,
just faith and push is all you need.
beyond the boundaries, lies your glory
which no one but you only can conquer.

Govind M Waswani

"Govind M Waswani, a 23-year-old from Nagpur, Maharashtra. He is penning down his quotes and thoughts since 2015 and on the page @livelovelaugh_lifegoals from 2017. He completed his graduation in B.pharmacy and currently working in TCS (Tata Consultancy Service). He developed a passion for writing when he realised it's beauty, it's precision. He thought writing is a mean of communication with utmost clarity. Writing was never a profession but somehow become a passion for him as he loves meaningful communications.

Insta handle :
@livelovelaugh_lifegoals
@Govind_waswani"

Life Lessons For Twenties.

You will lose a lot of people and that's what you cannot control. Goodbyes are difficult because only a few friends will genuinely care about you, In the end.

It's totally okay to feel complicated and insecure sometimes. Life is not perfect and things are temporary. You will have a hard time before you finally accept this.

Things hurt, people change, priorities get replaced. I know you hate losing the people you gave all your love to, but what's gone once will hardly comeback.

Finding your true love In real life takes a lot of efforts. Relationship are not easy. But until you will find your right person, please don't settle for the wrong one.

Not everything will work the way you want. You will make mistakes, mess things up and and get hurt badly but remember only you are responsible for your own happiness.

It is better to have only 2 real friends than having 20 fake people in your life. And that's a two way street. Invest your time in people who show that they value you.

Stop judging people, you've no idea what the other person is hiding behind that happy face. Be kind, we all are learning and also trying to get better with me.

Keep your self respect before everything else, no one or nothing more important than treating yourself right. No Matter how long it takes, learn to walk away."

Don't Lose Them Away

I was walking down the line
On the way I never knew,
Many people came into my life
But the loved ones were only few.

Not everyone you meet
Wishes good for you,
And it's a lesson to learn
Because word's can't be true.

Among the hidden faces
If you got some real one ?
Don't lose them away
Because they aren't easy to earn."

People's

The worst part of growing up is that you loose people to time and distance and there's nothing you can do about it. Some friendship are able to stand against all the odds while others simply fade away.

I wouldn't lie, but I do miss my people sometime. I remembered how close we used to be and how nice things were between us untill I'm eventually slapped back to the reality.

Because I realized that we've grown apart and that distance won over us. We barely talk now and the vibe doesn't exist anymore. Deep down we both know and understand that we are not good for each other.
This is how it feels : you have mixed feelings when you think of them because a part of you is not willing to believe that it's not the same anymore. You are hit by an unusual feeling which brings back to the memories.

You don't know how to stopped this because this feelings wears off on its own. You cannot fast forward the process, you meet them in your mind, things start replaying in front of your eyes. And honestly thats Okay.

It's makes you understand the fact that you can know someone more than they know themselves and still lose that bond with time, Life happens. People change. Priorities get replaced you can't help it.

The best thing you can do is move on with life because trust me, you'll find better people. You'll make friends who will never walk away or make you sad all the time.

To all the lessons, the memories, the tears, the pain, the mistake and the people I've lost. Thank you for being in my life. You've made me strong and changed me forever. "

Monika

She is pursuing bsc biotechnology from banathali vidyapith. Her hobby is to write something. And she is inspired by one of her classmate.

Life Is A Paint

Life is like a piece of art
It required lots of heart
Choose your paint brushes
Take your time and avoid the rush

Before you paint choose your theme don't affraid to follow your dream
It's alright, to make mistake
Your painting is real its not fake

Life is full of challenges
So look at the paint don't be crying being again keep on trying
Your painting is never fully completed

Sometimes in life we make good choice and sometimes not as good
I think that is ok to make mistake we learn from them.But also mistake are a part of life that make us real genuine human being

Nicky Bharat

Nicky Bharat, an Indian born, Her birth to a Jain Joint family has imbibed qualities of working together as a team, understanding multitude natures of people and remain grounded to values and founding principles. Education with reputed schools and college inculcated the sense of standing up for herself to become a fine woman with strength and courage, 14 years of Professional life have strongly shaped her personality and skills. Her cross cultural marriage over the decade has given the ability to assimilate into dwelling to new environments with ease. Being a Mother skilled her to work smoothly through roller coasters, work with precision and patience in times of crisis, time and resource management and most important to have compassion and give before you take ideology and attitude

When The World Turned Black & White

A day we dint think existed, here is a world standing still
A day we did not predict, or the technology anticipate at will
When the illusion of a multicolored fairy tale called life
Suddenly reads "THE END" and turns black and white.
And you wonder if it is the end of the chapter or the book,
The search is on! It is time we look beyond the hook.
Who is responsible for what we have no control on?
Who can we blame? Can we find balance again?
Puppets of a giant mistake, did manifestation win this game?
As we introspect the clearer it is, what we sow is what we reap,
This is the truth; we must trust and take the leap!
We remember the days when we woke up as bright as the Sun,
The nights we rested peacefully like the giant calm Earth.
As owners of the space between the Earth and Sun
Who is that intruding this colored fun?
To color it back we need to dig deeper than our Mind,
This is part which begins the grind
We chased everything for the boon,
Painted colors to not get doomed,
It's now just down to what we are, and we are not!
Why do we feel so tired to investigate?
So much that we just think and think and lay!
Searching for the dreams with the perfect colors,
oh! Dear Come, back now it is getting clear!
We are the power; we are the vibe!
Now we resonate with the Black & white.
Putting pieces together is not a fairy tale,
Oh! Yes, it is true the colors do fade away!
Putting the pieces of the puzzle,
Corners are the parts we are told,

Fills in between with those that our mind beholds,
In the center lies the finish, one which comes only from within!
A point has no dimensions, but just a position!
We are the point we define our spot,
In this universal space, we are just a dot,
To move closer to the truth is all we have got.
Now the power seems to rise, the gas solidifies,
The book still at THE END, then how are we seeing the abundance?
How did we see color in this Black & White?
With ourselves how did we unite?
With power comes its ego, like with light comes its shadow,
Now the color must exist with the Black and White,
Like the two sides of a coin tossing around to decide
Is this answer right or wrong, it is a choice to which you belong!
In this world of questions and doubts
Your only judge is the black and white!
For when you will answer to the within,
Fearless you are for any colored skin!

Samiksha

A girl who is teacher by profession and loves to do writing by passion..she belongs to bathinda in punjab...except writing she loves to do click pictures and cooking too...from the past 2 years writing is something like her best friend..weather she is sad or happy..angry or over exicted..she do write and it gives her immense pleasure and satisfaction...besides writing...she is also working for Ashmann Foundation NGO which also works for widows females and their education...keeping always postive attitude she want to aware society.
instagram handle..... @samiksha79

My Fully Engerised New Room

Strange time can lead us to new discoveries about ourselves. Things that may surprise us like to dreams of new rooms in a house is often an indication of this. New rooms in a house in a dream can relate to areas of our lives where we are discovering new skills, abilities or strengths within ourselves. while we make feel we know who we are and what we are capable of Dreams of new rooms invite us to open our minds to the possibilities that we have even greater potential than we thought. New rooms are like extension of ourselves. dreams of new rooms invite us to look at what with thought were our limitations and to recognise that we can move beyond them. Opening the doors and windows can be a symbol of being open to new ideas and opportunities coming to our house.so too can a fresh and revitalising and energy flow through our lives.if we met people there and are welcome in this can be a particular symbol of reaching and getting in touch with the new aspects of our personality. if we unlock the door to enter, this can be a symbol of ""Unlocking our potential"". It is not unusual to feel a little nervous as we first discovered these new rooms after all with think we know ourselves quite well so to suddenly stumble over new capabilities within ourselves can make a little getting used to. but if we react to this room with fear and locked the door or decide to keep the room secret this could indicate a sense of shame or a concern that we cannot let others see the real person that we are in. Many cases this can lead to stress and frustration .

So always remember:-

1. keep choosing new activity either it is big or small
2. second fantasize about how would you feel if your goals were reach but remember to also enjoy the journey

3. Remember times when you tried something new and learnt from your experience always take the will power of risks

4. stay around the people who make you feel like Sunshine

5. eliminate any one who is going to hold you back from becoming a better person because your time on this earth is limited and you better make time and space for people who really care for you

6. Lastly you deserve to be loved not just any love but Deep and mad love because you are special.

You are very much special and make yourself a Priority because ""Energy Never Lie""."

Mariya Suryavanshi

She is an undergraduate student who loves to write.She recently published her first book "Bitter Coffee-Dairy of Alina". She likes to sing and draw as well.

आशाना

यू तो ख्वाईश थी, इस ज़ेहन में,
तुम सबको अजबेर कर लेना।
पहली उस मुलाकात को, उन यादों में,
मजूल कर भर लेना।।

चाहे इस क्लब को याद नहीं
वह पहला दिन हमारा।
मासिवा, फिर भी हमारी वह शरारतें
हमें भूलना ना है गवारा।।

शुरुवात के वह पल जो थे, तब ना थे हम
दोस्त ऐसे इतने भी पास।
मगर जब हुए मुनासिब एक-दुजे के
तर्ज़-ऐ-अमल से, तो रिश्ता बना कुछ खास।।

तुम सब गेर थे दुनिया के नजर में, फिर
भी मेरे कुछ यू अपने हुए।
साथ जो मिला मुझे तुम सबका, तो
हकीकत मेरे यू अपने हुए।।

जब वह वक्त आया, खुद पर जब मैं
हिमायत ना कर पाई।
तब यारो, तुम सब ने हौसला अफजाई दी मुझे
मुझपर ये इनायत करके ।।

कभी नाराज हुए हम, कभी थे
मन में कुछ गीले-शिख्वे।

फिर भी हमारे खुदी को हमने रख अलग,
कहा-""चलो फिर एक बार हम कहानी लिखे"" ।।

शुक्राना चाहे मैं जितना भी करू, इस
ज़ेहन के लिए कम तार ही होगा।
दुनिया कहे गेर भी, यह दोस्ती है हमारी,
किसी को ना देंगे हक चढ़ाने को वह कर तार का जोगा ।।

I...

I was waiting for someone,
for whom I don't know
I was seen to be desperate,
sitting still onto the window

Was I trying to find out
why was I sad?
Why did I woke up suddenly,
being freakingly mad?

Neither my heart, nor my brain
none knew the answer
My feelings, my emotions
were just like a wild bouncer

Then I remembered, the people
I care for, the people I love
So, I picked my phone up, called a person
whom I see as a frove

Talking was not something,
I was yet ready for
But still that laughter brusted, when
my frove told I am a teary store

Making up things are what my
thoughts have had fun with
Hence, I looses everyone, along by
my bitter tongue, my gun teeth

Yes, I got up with the reason, reason

why was I waiting
My bestie told me, I was that reason,
the one who was letting

I so started checking up messages
from all loved one's, their status
Some wrote how they missed me,
but then too, my heart was just stratus

I no more wanted to stay together,
as I enjoyed being lonely
Yet one person, my frove, he pushed me to
himself, connected as if bonely

I have decided not to have anymore hopes,
being alone is the best choice
Having a frove is enough for me, no more
games of family-friends, just being me is my voice"

Samiran Bhatt

18 मार्च 1997 में जन्मे समीरण का बचपन से ही कथा, कविता एवं निबंध लेखन में रुचि रही। उन्होंने विद्यालय स्तर पर समय-समय पर इसमे प्रतिभाग किया एवं पुरस्कार भी जीते। उन्होंने अपने बीटेक की पढ़ाई जी बी पंत कृषि एवं प्रौद्योगिकी विश्वविद्यालय से की और फिर एमटेक आईआईटी भुवनेश्वर से पूर्ण किया। लेखन के अलावा देशाटन में भी उनकी रुचि है जिसमें उन्हें अपने देश की कला और संस्कृति के बारे में जानना काफी पसंद है। भविष्य में उनका उद्देश्य समाज सेवा कर देश को प्रगति के पथ पर बढ़ने में अपना योगदान देने का है।

कठिन परिश्रम का फल - जिंदगी का मधुर एहसास

जीवन एक प्रतियोगिता है और इसके तमाम संघर्ष हमें मजबूत बनाते हैं, ऐसा हमें बचपन में सिखाया जाता है। पर यह संघर्ष हर किसी के जीवन में अलग रूप लेकर आता है, किसी का कम होता है तो किसी का ज्यादा, पर होता सब का है । ऐसी ही एक कहानी है आशीष की, अगर आप आज आशीष को जानते हो तो आप कहेंगे कितना बड़ा आदमी है पर आपने आदमी को आज देखा है, उसके कल के संघर्ष को नहीं।

आशीष का जन्म एक किसान परिवार में हुआ था, बचपन में ही एक बार उसके गांव के खेतों में वहां के डीएम दौरा करने आए थे। उन्होंने किसानों की काफी मदद की उनका काफी उत्साह वर्धन किया और उनको कठिन परिश्रम करके अनाज उत्पन्न करने का आभार भी व्यक्त किया। उनकी इसी विनम्रता और समाज में इज्जत और रुतबे की वजह से आशीष के मन में उस दिन एक बात ठहर गई, कि उसे भी डीएम बनना है। धीरे-धीरे यह बात आशीष की मेहनत में झलकने लगी। आशीष दोस्तों से, अध्यापकों से, हर जगह जब भी मौका मिले डीएम बनने का रास्ता पूछता और धीरे-धीरे आशीष ने अपनी सामाजिक ज्ञान को भी सुधारा । आशीष पढ़ने में काफी तेज था तो घर वालों और अध्यापकों ने, सब ने उसे कहा कि 11वीं में तो विज्ञान ले ले आगे काफी स्कोप है। आशीष ने भी सोचा, हां ले ही लेता हूं विज्ञान, ज्यादा अंतर थोड़ी आएगा। आशीष ने विज्ञान ले ली, ग्यारहवीं के बाद बारहवीं आई और उसने जेईई का फॉर्म भरा। बुद्धि तेज होने की वजह से आशीष का इंजीनियरिंग में चयन हो गया। उसे राज्य के विख्यात कॉलेज में एडमिशन मिला। वहां उसके काफी दोस्त बने और उसने काफी कुछ सीखा। समाज के बारे में उसे ज्यादा जानकारी तो नहीं थी पर वहां कॉलेज जाकर उसे कई नई चीजों का पता चला। उसके कॉलेज का दोस्त विशाल भी आईएएस की तैयारी

कर रहा था तो दोनों की काफी अच्छी मित्रता हुई। विशाल ने आशीष को काफी अच्छा गाइड किया कि कैसे उसे तैयारी करनी है, आशीष ने भी तभी से शुरूआत कर ली अपने इस सफर की।

बीटेक के 4 सालों का मानो पता ही ना चला। दोस्तों की चकाचौंध, सीनियर की रैगिंग सब कुछ एक प्रवाह की तरह निकल गया। अबकी बार भी घरवालों ने कहा बीटेक के बाद प्लेसमेंट ले ले, पर आशीष का निश्चय इस बार अटल था कि उसे आईएएस बनना है और यह बात उसने अपने हृदय में बिठा ली । उसने अपने घर वालों को 1 साल बाद नौकरी लगने का वादा किया और फिर अपनी तैयारी में जुट गया। पर विधि का विधान हमेशा हमारे पक्ष में नहीं होता। पहली बार मैं आशीष का प्री का एग्जाम ही क्लियर नहीं हो पाया। आशीष निराश तो हुआ पर उसने अपनी हताशा को चंद पलों में ही निकाल दिया और दुबारा दृढ़ निश्चय और संकल्प के साथ तैयारी में जुट गया। अगली बार उसने बहुत मेहनत की, प्री एग्जाम भी क्लियर किया लेकिन अबकी बार मेंस एग्जाम में रुक गया। काफी हताश हुआ क्योंकि अब घरवालों की दी गई अवधि भी समाप्त हो चुकी थी। घरवालों से काफी नौकरी का प्रेशर भी आ रहा था पर उसने इस बार भी उन्हें मना लिया और दोबारा तैयारी में जुट गया। अबकी बार उसका प्री के बाद मेंस भी क्लियर हुआ लेकिन अब इसे फूटी किस्मत कहो या कुछ और उसका इस बार का सफर इंटरव्यू में थम गया। अबकी बार वो टूट चुका था, पूरी तरह से हताश हो चुका था, तो उसने अलग-अलग नौकरी के फॉर्म भरने शुरू कर दिये और साथ ही साथ अपनी तैयारी भी जारी रखी। उसने अन्य काफी एग्जाम निकाले, पर उसके लिए जो सबसे महत्वपूर्ण एग्जाम था उसमें वह कभी प्री में, कभी मेंस तो कभी इंटरव्यू में बाहर हो जाता। हताशा के इस मोड़ पर उसने अपने सपने को दफना दिया और पुलिस में भर्ती ले ली।

आशीष अपनी नौकरी में भी अपने जीवन के दफन हुए सपने को मिटा नहीं पा रहा था। वहां पर उसके बॉस कहा करते थे कि ""यदि आप कभी विफल होकर खड़े होते हैं तो आप मूर्ख हैं और अगर आप अपनी विफलता का कारण समझ कर खड़े होते हैं तो आप बुद्धिमान है।"" यह बात आशीष के मन में ठहर गई उसने सोचा कि उसने इतनी बार कोशिश तो की पर उसने कभी यह नहीं सोचा कि उसका सिलेक्शन क्यों नहीं हो रहा है। उसने जाना और लिखा कि उसकी कमजोरियां क्या है और उन सब पर उसने बारीकी से काम किया और दोबारा एक नई ऊर्जा के साथ जॉब के साथ-साथ ही परीक्षा की तैयारी करने लगा। जॉब काफी व्यस्त थी फिर भी वह जितना हो सके पढ़ाई के लिए समय निकाल लेता था। इसी बीच उसे पता चला कि विशाल का पीसीएस में चयन हो गया है और इसी खुशी को उसने अपने आप को और बेहतर बनाने का कारण बना दिया।

इस बार अपना आखिरी अटैम्पट होने के कारण वह पूरे जी जान से तैयारी में जुट गया। जब इस बार तैयारी कर रहा था तो उसके मन में एक सनक थी कि उसे अबकी बार आईएएस बनना है, कैसे भी किसी भी हालत में। उसने प्री निकाला, मेंस निकाला और इंटरव्यू भी अच्छा दिया। अब वह दिन आ चुका था जब रिजल्ट आया, वह डरा हुआ था, उसके अंदर रिजल्ट देखने की हिम्मत नहीं आ रही थी। तभी उसके फोन की घंटी बजी, उसने उठाया और विशाल ने कहा आशीष तेरा नाम लिस्ट में ऑल इंडिया रैंक 11 पर आया है। आशीष को विश्वास ही नहीं हुआ, वह बोला विशाल जरा मेरा रोल नंबर चेक कर तो। विशाल ने फिर रोल नंबर चेक किया और रोल नंबर मैच हो गया। अब तो आशीष फूला ना समा रहा था। घर वालों को जब आशीष ने बताया तो उसके माता पिता की आंखों से खुशी के आंसुओं की बूंदे गिर गयी। अपने परिवार में यह खुशी देखकर और अपने परिश्रम का ये फल पाकर आशीष को अलग ही सुख की अनुभूति हो रही थी।

आज भी आशीष जब भी उस क्षण को याद करता है तो उसे वह अश्रु बूंदे और वो खुशी उसकी जिंदगी के सबसे मधुर एहसास बन कर आती रहती है ।

सत्य घटना पर आधारित "

Ananya Kumar

Ananya is a poet who focuses on women as her subject of interest.

Shawl

The last time I saw my nani, I asked her if she had a spare shawl. It gets cold when I study at night. She laughed and handed me her own shawl, blue with fine kaani embroidery. Keep it, she said, iron it and wear it. She offered another but I refused, said I'll be back home in April anyway. I told her about a shawl that was supposed to cost five lakh rupees, so fine it was thinner than paper. We laughed together about it. I call my mom and ask her about home these days. I call my nani and ask her if she's alright. I'm quarantined away from home so I keep myself busy with my relatives here. I wash the dishes, I watch new shows. I try to not think about the blue shawl tucked in my hostel room, waiting for me."

Coffee

I poison myself in an attempt to change every piece of me
So that I'm no longer the girl who loved her
I sing loudly in long showers and cry over soap operas
I stop using my cute voice because she told me she likes it
I tell everyone ""its complicated""
But is it? Do I truly change?
I talk about how everyone wants me
But I never mention how in love with everyone I am
I talk about not being wanted
But the truth lies in the heart of me that
I'll cling to this love like a cup of coffee
I'll drink it down, bitter at the end and nearly poison at the last sip
Drink it as it gets colder and colder
Until the steamy cup turns lukewarm
Until she cuts me off from my urges
I'll stay"

Sunlight

Sunlight hits your hands
And they're moving pictures
If only all the wonders of the world could compare
To your hand coming to grasp mine
I keep looking at your fingers
See them stained with henna for a moment and my heart stops
I force it to beat again as your hands hold my face
Bring me closer as my cheeks burn
Hands tangle in my dark hair and stay there
I laugh at something and you look at me
The rapture of the depths drags me under
As your fingers tickle my scalp
Come home to me"

Ankita Hundekar

She's Ankita Hundekar from Karnataka. She is studying bachelor of tourism. She believes that through her piece of writing she can inspire millions of lives. She has participated in 13 Anthologies and currently writing one! She believes words can outlive everything

Hey Dear !

It feels good to be your friend..
And make you realize you always have a hand ;
To be your strength..
And let you know your Worth!

Of cloudless dark climes ..
I will let you have good vibes..
Despite odds, i will make you feel better ..
Happiness is all ,that I assure!

I will never complain...
As you are mine;
I will be the hope in your dark ..
Making sure that you spark !

I will let you heal...
All you really need is zeal;
Like a light in the dark..
I will let you have the good remarks..!

Experience As A Writer!

Knowing the agony of lows in life ..
With so many strifes;
It feels good to pen down my pain..
Because I know I have to gain !

Listening to the problem of reader..
Making them feel better;
I know healing words are all you need ..
Making you feel better is a good deed !

Being an angelic soul..
Making sure you dwell ;
Writers,never blighter..
But will make you feel brighter!

They are here to make you win..
By never letting you down ;
A good message bearer...
Also ,a problem solver!

To My Favorite Person..!

You are the hope in the dark..
Like a twinkling spark ;
When ,life was just filled with remorse..
To find joy,you became an evident source!

You are my favorite pair of eyes that I look into ..
You are the only one whom I talk to ;
In the gloomy world you are my charm..
All I need is your hug ,that's so warm !

You are my deepest weakness..
My only sweetness;
Of cloudless climes and starry skies..
Our togetherness, nor heaven denies!

My love will not be lost in the air..
It will be till the forever;
I neither wish nor complain..
I will just be there with you even in the rain !"

Sanamsmita Sahu

Sanam is a new, budding writer, trying to prove her credentials in this platform. Generally a short story writer, and moreover a quote maniac, always grasped for the reality under fantasy. Currently she is a student of computer application but she respects highly for these creative phrases.

Remedy

Murkiness of the layered darkness
Engulfed her tiny form flashing all bleak
Weary eyes drooping over sloping her to the cold tile surface
Clinging to her shaky knee she placed her
Neglected head.
Devoured by the fierce winter, she taken aback
Yeah!! She was cooped up within her own fears
Dreaded over the thought of peril to them
Metals clanking shaking her only soul
Beaming tears making her drown in her own grief
Grabby hands Scouring for the exit
Chaotic brain of her is now going all mute
Pain was unbearable, eyes were damp
Until Streaks of light hit her with care
With the music of love, They came.
Making the number lucky 7,a boon for her
Clasping her hands, giving the priceless peck on forehead, the elder made her smile again
Dimpled boy giving her hope, bringing her to the sunshine, she craved
Gleaming his gummy bear, the other made her strong filling her with savage
Escorting to the stage of passion, they let her live
Teaching the purple love, being with her in every thick n thin, they made her life giggle forgetting the wounds.
"Fairy Tales are Fake!! "But, she tasted exception!
Angels of care to tranquilize her pain
As the REMEDY of her nightmares
Soulmate of her Dreams to make her paradise, a FOREVER long!!

Ashutosh Kumar

He is a student and enjoys writing. From Muzaffarpur,Bihar

Belief In Yourself

Experience is defined as the knowledge or skill made by seeing or doing something. Experience is the thing which can not be made in a day. But once made it's going to be with us for lifetime. Oscar Wilde had said- ' Experience is the hardest teacher. It gives you the test first and the lesson afterwards.' His words are absolutely right. We never know what is going to happen when we do something for the first time. Although, when we perform that activity we gain the experience of doing so. Let me give you my example, I was very scared how to do rappelling during one of my tour. So, somehow I completed that. After that, I got excited to do it again as I understood how to do it and did better than first time. We have also heard about many people who succeeded in their life due to vast experience they had made. That's why experience has a great role in our life. It's not always necessary to do the things to gain experience there various other options too. We can see someone performing the activity or hear from person who have performed it regarding that. It is often said that as we grow up, we become more experienced. Why is it so? Because as we become old we come across to many new situations and we handle them. The things which are new for youngsters, the elder people have already passed that stage. So, they are albe to provide the solution instantly.

In my 16 years of life, I have come across my ups and downs. And more I have to come across. Thus, I am here going to tell one of my experience of life which I have made till now. It's seems to very simple but always had a great impact on my life. I would say from my experience up to now that never ever lose your hope until the last minute. Yes, I am talking about faith in oneself. We should always have faith in ourselves. It's not the thing to be applied upon games only rather it is to be implemented in our life. It was the faith of Dashrath Manjhi(The Mountain Man) in himself only with which he carved a path between hills.

It's my personal experience that we should never lose hope till the last minute. I was in standard 5th and the school in which I studied used to conduct monthly test. So, for revision I was habitual of waking up early. A few times, I was not able to wake up or if woke up then late. Thus, after that I used to get very much irritated and frustrated. I just used to get angry and went back to bed. At that time my mother was there to make me understand that you are still left with some time. And you should utilise it at it's fullest. She always said to me belief in yourself and you will do well in your exams.At that time, I was habitual to think my mother tells me so to just sympathise me. Although, I realised this later on in my life. It's not the only instance which gave me experience that belief in yourself rather other occasions also when I understand this. After that I left worrying upon the bad time or just thinking of something bad happened to me. As the ultimate thing which I need is peace and happiness. Infact we all want these things in our life. We generally gets disappointed when something doesn't goes/work in our favour. In present day, we all run after success and not bother about other things. However, we should do hardwork to achieve our goals. And also live in the moment and enjoy the things around us. Achieving your goals like this has a separate feeling. This is not impossible just we need to have faith in ourselves along with keeping our goal in mind.

Believing in yourself is the best thing that one can have. As it don't allow us to think about leg pullers comments and the perception of what other people will think about me too. This should be the sentiment of people. This point of view is very important to get success in life. Also, belief in oneself is the best motivation. No one can be able to motivate you for any task until you don't have faith in you to do it. Thus, belief in yourself and do well...."

Anjali Singh

Anjali Singh is second year BAF student she plays football she is kind hearted she loves music she is a big time foodie. She likes challenges, she is a kind of person who sets a goal and challenges herself to achieve it. She has discovered how good she is with words she comes up with as we say "shero shayari" while cooking while listening to music and so on. In coming future she is planning to enroll herself in creative writing to groom her writing skills.

(1)

Life is a box of mystery.. It's a problem with solution, it will give you clue to find your path n sometime it will become all puzzle to solve. But once you will learn how to play, it will become more n more interesting game to play. And at the end it will give you it's treasure (death eternal way to live.)to live in another way..!!

(2)

Life is like a novel Birth is it's first lesson, Love comes in it like a mid portion,
And continuous till death.

(3)

Life is black and white,
You be my black, I'll be your white,
And together we will create a beautiful life.

Priyanshu Bhatt

प्रांसूर्य सैनिक स्कूल घोड़ाखाल के पूर्व छात्र है। उनका जन्म 22 अप्रैल 2003 को हुआ था। वह वर्तमान में एक रक्षा आकांक्षी हैं। वह एक लेखक भी हैं और विभिन्न अवसरों पर अपने लेख देते हैं। वह कविता भी पसंद करते हैं और "पोएटिक बाबा" के नाम से एक यू-ट्यूब चैनल चलाते हैं। वह नौसेना में शामिल होने की इच्छा रखते है।

जीवन में खुशी की अनुभूति का मार्ग

तो कहानी शुरू होती है तब, जब इंसान इस धरती पर आया था। उसके बाद धीरे-धीरे हमारी सभ्यता फैली और हमने नए - नए आविष्कारों के दम पर अपने आप को इस धरती पर एक प्रमुख प्रजाति के रूप में स्थापित किया। यह कहानी जिसे आज हम जी रहे हैं , वह सदियों पुरानी है। पर अगर हम आज का परिपेक्ष देखें तो हम देखेंगे कि हमें इस कहानी के सम्मान में काफी कमी दिखेगी। जिस सम्मान कि मैं बात कर रहा हूं वह सम्मान मात्र इज्जत करना नहीं है, बल्कि हमारी पुरखों की विरासत को बरकरार रखना है। बरकरार रखने से मेरा तात्पर्य है की हमें इस जीवन का आदर करना है। हमारे पुरखों ने काफी मेहनत से न जाने किन हालातों में अपना जीवन गुजारा पर इस सभ्यता को आगे बढ़ाया। उन्होंने कभी भी इस जीवन का अनादर नहीं किया, हमेशा जीवन को भगवान का तोहफा समझा। उनको जो कुछ भी मिला, उसी में वे खुश रहे। लेकिन आज ना जाने, सब कुछ होते हुए भी मनुष्य तृप्त नहीं है।

जिंदगी जीना और जिंदगी खुशी से जीना दोनों में काफी अंतर होता है। जिंदगी तो हर कोई जी लेता है पर खुशी से जीना हर किसी को नसीब नहीं होता। अगर हम खुशी से जीना चाहते हैं तो हमें अपने अंदर खुशी ढूंढनी होगी। अगर हम सोचे कि हमारी लालसा पूरी होते ही हमारे जीवन में ख़ुशी की बहार आ जाएगी तो ऐसा नहीं होगा। एक लालसा दूसरी लालसा को जन्म देती है और इसी तरह यह सिलसिला अंत तक चलता है, अंत यानी कि मृत्यु। मनुष्य चाहे कितना ही गरीब हो लेकिन हर किसी के जीवन का अपना महत्व होता है। हमें अपनी पूरी कोशिश से इस महत्व को ढूंढना और उसे पूरा करना चाहिए।

हमारी सोच मात्र जात-पात, पैसा और तमाम सामाजिक दायरो से ऊपर है, बस हम उस ऊपर के माले पर जाना पसंद नहीं करते। और यही कारण है कि हम खुश नहीं रह पाते। कहने का तात्पर्य यह है कि हमें रोज मेहनत तो करनी चाहिए अपने आप को और बेहतर बनाने के लिए, लेकिन हमारी मेहनत सिर्फ पैसे तक सीमित नहीं रहनी चाहिए। दुनिया में पैसे के बिना कुछ नहीं होता, पर पैसा ही सब कुछ नहीं है। हमें इस सोच को लेकर आगे बढ़ना चाहिए। तभी हम मेहनत करें वह खुद को बेहतर बनाने के लिए रोज़ कोशिश करें।

जीवन बहुत मजेदार है, बस हमें मजे से जीना है। तो संक्षेप मैं अगर कहा जाए तुम्हारे जीवन में पहले से ही खुशियां हैं बस तुम उसे देख नहीं पा रहे हो। जीवन खुशियों का एक एहसास है बस हमें अपना नजरिया बदलना होगा।

आंख मिचौली खेलें उन बच्चों में न जाने क्या चमक थी,
नादान थे वह, उन्हें इस बात की क्या समझ थी।
पर उनकी आंखों में खुशियों का आभास होता था,
उनको देखकर ही सामने वाले के मन में हर्ष का एहसास होता था।
10 साल बाद उनकी खुशी तुलना में बदल गई,
न जाने ज्यादा अमीर बनने की प्रतियोगिता, उनके मन में कैसे ठहर गई।
काश इनका मन तृप्त होता,
उन्हें पता होता,
कि अगर पैसे से ही खुशी मिलती तो आज हर सड़क पर खुशी का व्यापार होता।""

Kiran Gehlot

Kiran Gehlot (siya) has been writter as a passion. She provides many other gener for her page. Her educational background in Life science and Microbiology. Her writing skills may be confirmed independently on ||IG||Moonbow_words_dz page. She especially enjoys preparing different gener for her write ups which are challenging for every writter.

बीमारी

राख हुए सपने मेरे,
ख़ाक में मिल गया ख्वाबो का बसेरा,
तुम रहे करीब हमेशा,
दूर हो गया साथ तेरा,
खोना पड़ा तुझे एक राह में,
मिल गए तुम मंज़िल पर कहीं,
मिले बिछड़े और फिर ये दूरी आ गई,
जाने कोनसी बीमारी हमारे रिश्ते को खा गई,
तुम्हे खोने से लगा जो डर कभी,
वैसा फिर कभी हुआ ही नहीं,
तुम मिल गए फिर बड़ी मुद्दतो के बाद मुझे,
खुदा करे ये ख्वाब कभी टूटे ही नहीं...

ख़्वाबों का सफर

ख़्वाबों के आड़े मेरे रिश्ते आ गए,
कुछ बाहरी लोग मेरी ज़िन्दगी खा गए,
किसी ने नोची रूहे हमारी,
किसी ने चाहा जिस्म को नोचना,
इतना मिला दर्द के हम,
ज़िन्दगी से ही हार गए,
चीख चीख के सांसे रुकी,
और हमने वहीं दम तोड दिया,
कुछ लोगों ने कहा पराया,
और राह में साथ छोड़ दिया,
ख़्वाबों के सफर का ये कारवा,
हमने राह में ही छोड़ दिया,
कुछ बाहरी लोगो ने,
हमसे हमारी रूह को ही छीन लिया...

सफर

तड़पे जहां की खुशी के लिए,
ऐसी भी कोई बात नहीं,
तू ही गया किसी और का,
बेवफा तेरे ही साथ रही,
जिए वो सफर ज़िन्दगी का,
जिसमे तेरी बात नहीं,
अब बस भी करे आप,
तड़पाना छोड़ो भी,
तेरे लिए रोएंगे क्या सोचा,
अरे बस भी करो,
तुमने इतनी भी कोई खास बात नहीं..."

Kritika Sharma

"Kritika Sharma is from twin city Ambala, Haryana.
Writing calms her soul.She can express every emotion through words. Words are her power. She can transform every feeling into words. Words pop up into her mind after seeing every living and even non living thing. She can play with words very well.

Life

A complex mixture of happy sad experiences,
Another name for adjustments and compromises,
A complete season full of beautiful and ugly moments,
Our life is a body deodorised by feelings named scent,
Childhood is like a rainbow,
No worries no problems face always filled with glow,
Teenage teaches a lot of lessons,
Love betrayal still this phase is a blessing,
Adulthood is lost in career issues,
A melancholy of dejection and mind full of blues,
Elderly age a span of responsibilities,
Old age is similar to childhood but with seniority,
Life should be treated with care but should be carefree,
We should enjoy the small moments as it's the little things in life I strongly agree..

Rainbow

Raindrops fall on earth,

Beautiful hopes take birth,

Rain is a gift given by clouds,

Positivity and optimism singing aloud,

These clouds when combine with sunlight,

A charming rainbow makes my heart skip a beat,

Seven colours convey seven different messages,

The mesmerizing view steals away my tragedies,

Violet is the colour of creation,

It showers of strengthening every relation,

This colour connects us to the spiritual values,

Embracing and enhancing the sky's view,

Indigo colour conveys wisdom and integrity,

It is a symbol of tradition I totally agree,

This colour is pure just as a mother's love,

How lovely it look embedded in a curve,

Blue colour is a symbol of stability,

As calm as the sky and the sea,

This colour is the reflection of loyalty and heaven,

It removes every thought of separation,

Green is the colour of safety and nature,

It symbolizes harmony and expenditure,

Green is the colour of an emotional mind,

It gives tranquility and is divine,

Yellow is the colour of enlightenment,

That favours all the people stay united,

The most luminous colour I feel,

Rainbow is magnificent because of this,

Orange the combination of red and yellow,

It makes me filled with joy never let me feel low,

It reflects the sign of fascination,

The most vibrant colour fills me with enthusiasm,

The colour which is leader of all,

Red colour picks me up whenever I am about to fall,

The colour of love and affection,

Red colour symbolizes immense pleasure,

How can one not be mesmerized by this beauty,

The vibrant rainbow looks like ice cream tootie fruity,

I want to taste this cluster of colours,

Wanna get lost in this miracle of nature,

One should learn to glow like a rainbow,

One should understand when two souls combine they can make the whole world glow,

Rainbow teaches us the power of love,

The delightful creation of god makes me blow"

Sourabh Sinoy

Sourabh sinoy,currently he is purseuing the cource of B.tech Marine
Engineering from Indian Maritime University,chennai.
National Throwball player.
Reading and writing is his passion,aim to publish a book.
Also,he is running a youtube chennal,'conatus of poetry',which is related to poetry and philosophical thoughts.Instagram page@conatus of poetry.
Insta/fb-@sourabh_sinoy

अंतचेतना, जिंदगी और जिंदगी का सबसे बड़ा एहसास!

मैं अपने पैदा होने के पहले भी था
और अपने अंत के बाद भी रहूंगा।
अपने पैदा होने के पहले,
मे किसी की मन की तरंगों में था
और अपने मर जाने के बाद
किसी की यादों की तिजोरी में रहुंगा।

फूल के मुरझा जाने के बाद,उसकी रंगों की चमक फीकी पड़ने लगती है,उसकी महक हवा में धुंधली होने लगती है,
पर मन की तिजोरी में वह चमक और वह महक हमेशा चमकती महकती रहती है।फूल के मुरझा जाने ना होने के बाद भी उसकी होने की गवाही हमारे मन में बैठा वह चमक वह महक देता रहता है।
दिन हो या रात पूर्णिमा या अमावस चांद हर वक्त होता है, उसकी चांदनी नहीं होती।कई बार लोग होकर भी नहीं होते। कई बार लोग नहीं होते पर साथ होते।
मेरे प्रारंभ और अंत की अंतराल मात्र भर मेरी जिंदगी नहीं है। मैं,मेरे पैदा होने के पहले भी था और मेरे मृत्यु के बाद भी रहुंगा...मेरे पैदा होने के पहले,मैं किसी की मन की तरंगों में था और मेरे अंत के बाद किसी की यादों की तिजोरी में मौजूद रहूंगा।मेरे शरीर की हजारों कोशिका भले ही मिट्टी हो चुकी होगी। पर मेरी अंतचेतना की पुकार अभी भी अनंत ब्रह्मांड में कहीं थरथरा गुनगुना रही होगी।
कोई शोर नहीं होगा, कोई शांति नहीं होगी। कोई उजाला या अंधेरा नहीं होगा। कोई मोह नहीं ना कोई माया होगी। किसी से आसान नहीं होगी ना किसी से निराशा होगी।

ना किसी से सवाल होगा ना किसी को जवाब होगा,बस मैं और मेरी चेतना, चेतना से सवाल होगा, चेतना को ही जवाब होगा..
चेतना की हर एक पुकार मेरे वजूद को और निश्चित करेगी और करती रहेगी और करती ही रहेगी।

एहसास!

जिंदगी की हर एक पल कविता बुनती है। कविता की हर एक पंक्ति अहसास देती है। अस्मित ख़ुशी का एहसास, अनछुई सपनों का एहसास ,बीते हुए कल का एहसास ,टूटे हुए उम्मीद का एहसास ,हजारों शब्दो को स्याही से सजाने का एहसास उन शब्दों को हजारों बार पढ़ने और सुनाने का एहसास... पर जिंदगी की सबसे बड़ी एहसास क्या है?

जिंदगी की सबसे बड़ी एहसास खुद जिंदगी है और जिंदगी क्या है?

जिंदगी उन एहसासों की गठरी है जो हमने जिंदगी भर जिंदगी से जिंदगी को ही जानने के लिए लिया है।

चोर को चोरी करने के बाद का एहसास पुलिस को उस चोर के पकड़े जाने के बाद का एहसास सही या गलत हम सब के विवेक पर निर्भर करता है। पर एहसास सब की एक ही है। चाहे वह चोर की हो या पुलिस की।एहसास जो जिंदगी बनाता है जिंदगी जो एहसासों को समझने की जगह देती हैं..

कोई एहसास को परे रखकर जी नहीं सकता, नन्हीं जान से लेकर बाल अवस्था बालक से किशोर और फिर वृद्धावस्था हर एक क्षण मन को एक एहसास देती है

उम्मीद है मेरे कलम से निकली जिंदगी के एहसासों की कविता आपके मन को कुछ कुछ बताइए कि तो कुछ विचलित करेगी...

उम्मीद है यह चंद शब्द आपको कुछ सपने कुछ हकीकत से वाकिफ कराएंगी आपके जिंदगी मे एक छोटा सा एहसास को जोड़ने का काम करेगी।

धन्यवाद!

Gurdeep Kaur

"She lives in varanasi. Her Hobbies are Dance writing, cooking and traveling . Writting is her best hobby to explain inner view .

जो हम कह नहीं पाते कभी कभी वो लिखकर बयां करते हैं "

Instagram ID @gur.deep0000.

Facebook id gur.deep0000

जिन्दगी के कुछ अनकहे पल

ज़िन्दगी हमें हर पल मे कुछ न कुछ देती हैं,कभी खुशी तो कभी गम, कभी किसी का प्यार तो कभी किसी की नफरत, हर बार कुछ न कुछ देती हैं, पर इन सबको देने के लिए कभी -कभी वो हमसे कुछ छीन लेती है, जिसका हम कभी सोच भी नही सकते।

जब आपके पास सिर्फ ऐसा कोई इंसान रह जाता है, उस पर ही आपकी पूरी जिंदगी की पूरी उम्मीद हो, कोई उसको आपसे कहीं दूर ले जाये, पूरी खुशी की उम्मीद हो, कुछ जख्म ऐसे है, जिन्हें कभी भरा नहीं जाता, ऐसा ही हुआ कुछ मेरे साथ जब मुझे सबसे ज्यादा जरूरत थी,अपने परिवार मे पापा की वो मुझे छोड़ कर चले गये। क्यों कैसे कब बस ये सवाल समझने का मौका ही नहीं मिला।

वो प्यार पाने की आदत नहीं रही, वो 20 दिन ऐसे निकले ,अब तो पूरी उम्र उसी मे लग जाएगी।

ये दिन तो निकल गये, पर आप आज भी मेरे साथ आपका आशीर्वाद बनकर हमेशा साथ हो, मेरी हिम्मत बड़ी मे जीवन मे आगे बढी, और अपने आप को आगे बढाया आपके साथ, वहां तक अपने आप को जहाँ की आपने चाह रखी होगी।

आपके जाने के बाद मैंने हिम्मत न हारी, आपको हमेशा अपने पास पाया, आपकी वो एक बात कभी न भूल पाओगी,

""कभी अपने ऊपर घमंड मत करना,

करना तो सिर्फ अपनी मौत के वक्त करना, क्योंकि उस वक्त तुमको ये मौका मिलेगा नहीं।""

मैं इस दुनिया की भीड़ मे अकेले रह गयी, पर आपके आशीर्वाद के साथ आज मे अपनी जिन्दगी मे आगे बढ गयी पर आपकी जगह हमेशा मेरी याद मे ही हैं। मैं आपकी तस्वीर को निकाल कर देख नहीं सकती वो हिम्मत मुझ मे नहीं है, पर जीवन मे अपने सारे अधूरे काम किये।

आपकी याद वहीं रुक कर रह गयी है, इस हिस्से ने मुझे हिम्मत दी कुछ आगे करने की ,अपनी पहचान बनाने की और इस दुनिया के कुछ लोगों के मुंह पर थप्पड़ मारने की जिसने मुझे कमजोर समझा। आपके बिना जीना सीख लिया, आपको जान कर खुशी होगी, पर आपकी यादों से निकल पाना मेरे लिए कभी आसान नहीं।

जानते हैं अब आपको न देख पायेंगे,
फिर भी पता नहीं क्यों एक आस है,
आपके आने की,
ये दिल जानता है, कि झूठ है ये
पर फिर मानता नहीं।"

Akash Malhotra

"He is Akash Malhotra, a student from lucknow, Uttar Pradesh. Likes to express himself through his writings and wishes to bring some positive changes in society
Instagram id akash22malhotra
Facebook page 1)Respect girls
2) akash22malhotra"

यूँ मायूस ना हो!!

दुःख आया तो क्या हुआ?
यूँ मायूस ना हो
ये तो जीवन का दस्तूर है
कभी खुशी तो कभी गम है
उठो और आगे बढ़ो
ईश्वर का ध्यान
उन पर आस्था रखों
और संघर्ष जारी रखों
सच्चाई की राह मत छोड़ी अगर
तो मिलेगी ही कामयाबी एक दिन

अधोपतन की सीढ़ियाँ

बिना मेहनत शौहरत की लालसा
गैर स्त्री पर खराब नियत डालना
मासूमो को सताना
प्रेम में ना सुनने को अपनी तौहीन समझकर
बदले की भावना रखना
अहंकार में अंधे होकर
खुदको सर्वश्रेष्ठ समझने की भूल करना
ईश्वर को भूलकर
पैसे और विषयवस्तु का ही चिंतन करना
यही है खुदके सर्वनाश की
यही है खुदके अधोपतन की सीढ़ियाँ उतरना "

भारतीय समाज की विडम्बना

करतें है देवियों की पूजा
लेकिन परिवार में बेटी के जन्म से दुःखी होते हैं
लड़कियो के साथ दुष्कर्म हो तो
दोषियों को छोड़
पीड़ीत को दोषी ठहराते हैं
कभी उनके रहन-सहन पर
कभी उनके पहनावे पर उँगली उठाते हैं
लड़कियो को इंसान से ज्यादा वासना पूर्ति का साधन मात्र समझते हैं
कुछ समय तक कैंडल मार्च निकालकर फिर सब भूल जाते हैं
इक ओर जहाँ विकास की सीढ़ियाँ चढते जाते हैं
दूसरी ओर पूरे देश में कहीं न कहीं बलात्कार
किसी ना किसी मासूम के साथ हो रहा है
कब तक हम यूँही चुप रहेंगे इस बारें में
आखिर कब तक नारी जाति पर यूँ अत्याचार होता रहेगा
क्यू हम इन विषयों से बचते फिरते हैं
जब तक हम खुद ही बदलेंगे
तब तक कैसे ये कलंक भारतीय समाज से हट सकेगा?
आखिर कब कैसे लड़कियो को एक सुरक्षित सम्मानजनक
वातावरण इस देश में मिलेगा??
"

Sana Tabassum

"Sana Tabassum, is a budding writer. She currently works as a lecturer in Hyderabad. Apart from teaching she savour the flavours of books, movies & music.
She strongly believes that, "fortune favours those who attempt to take risks."
She found her passion for writing in 2018 & since then there is no looking back. Her poetry was also published in the college magazine.
She explores different genres & portrays her musings through quotes & poems.
Instagram Id @wordbeans
Her works can be read on:
https://www.yourquote.in/sana93tabassum"

A Life's Mystical Quest

As I wandered across the unfathomed path,
in peace I couldn't bath
at a hermit's abode I stationed,
and he revealed the secret of our devastation.
It's only the Temptation
that's the sole answer of all disappointment,
to which there's ain't no ointment.
and then, to the vales I headed.
Astonished with its tranquillity,
I yearned to lodge there forever.
In the meads, where there's so much peace,
the nature at its own self, dost not bother what so ever goes along...
I learnt the life's lesson,
it ain't matter where you belong...
it's only the nature's beauty that lasts long.

A City Tale

In the city of tales
I tracked your trails
wandering across the lanes
I prayed not to lose my sane
I hoped to find you somewhere
so I started looking in every square
the city filled with your air
and to live without you was quite unfair
my search continued and never stopped
to every door I shamelessly knocked
I still hope to meet you again
and trust me it's not an easy bargain.
"

Dreams Unfathomed

Sailing across my dreams
I reached the hidden shore,
where I strived to unlock a secret door
I wandered across and took glimpse of the beauty,
but something pulled me back and reminded me of my duty
my dream shattered as the reality reflected in
I hope to travel again in that trance,
where harsh realities are
things of past

Hues Of Life

Life has mysterious hues
sometimes pink
other times blue

night is the eternal companion
of the day
and so are mortals,
never departed with their peaks and troughs

lets sojourned in the withered land,
to learn our goofs
then begin a quest for an abode,
where courage is not blasphemed

Neeha Muneer

She's pursuing Bachelor of Technology in Computer Science stream. She's from Hyderabad. She's a Passionate Author as well as a Singer too! She likes Cooking. Her hobbies are reading Novels and listening to music. Publishing a Book was her dream

एक जिंदगी

ज़िंदगी....... नाम से ही पता चल रहा हैं की ये बहुत कीमती चीज़ है। हम अपने ज़िन्दगी में बहुत कुछ देख चुके हैं। न जाने कितने गलतियाँ किये है। पर खुदा हमेशा हमें माफ़ करके दूसरा मौका देता हैं। ज़िन्दगी से अगर कभी आपको नफरत होगी ना? तब दूसरों की ज़िन्दगी के तरफ मुड़ के देखिए। वो लाग आपसे ज़्यादा मेहनत कर रहे हैं, ज़िंदा रहने के लिये। शुक्र कीजिये की खुदा आपको एक अच्छी ज़िन्दगी दी है। जित्ना हैं उतने में ही खुश रहनी चहिये। कभी दूसरों को देखके मत जलना, क्यूँकि वह ऊपर वाला हर एक चीज़ जिसको जितना देना हैना, उसको उतना देके ही रहेग। आप जैसी ज़िन्दगी जीने के लिए बहुत लाग तडपते हैं। आपको तोह बेहतर ज़िन्दगी मिली है। हमेशा शुक्रिया अदा कीजिये। अगर आप कुछ गलती की हैं तोह जाने दीजिये न। आखिर इंसान ही तोह गलती करते है। दूसरों को भी माफ़ कीजिये। दो दिन की ज़िन्दगी हैं, पता नै कल उसकी जगह आप आगए तो? इसीलिए ज़िन्दगी न मिलेगी दोबारा!!!! हमेशा ख़ुशी ख़ुशी से बिताईये, दूसरों को खुश राखिये। उनकी ख़ुशी में तो हमारी ख़ुशी बस्ती है। ग़लतियों से कुछ सीख लीजिये। भगवान हमेशा जो कुछ भी करता हैं, हमारे भलाई के लिए ही करता हैना। जो कुछ भी हुआ सब हमारे भलाई के लिए ही हुआ करके आगे बढिये। शायद आपको उससे भी अच्छी नसीब लिखा होगा किसको पता! जो कोई भी आपका मदद करता हैं तो उसे कभी मत भूलना! एहसान चुकाना ही पड़ेगा! ऐसी ज़िन्दगी तोह एक तौफा है। न जाने खुदखुशी करके या फिर उदास होके आपका वक़्त और आपका कीमती ज़िन्दगी बर्बाद मत कीजिये।

हर पल ख़ुशी से बिताईये। हमेशा ख़ुशी बाटिये :)"

Roopali Purohit

"Roopali is an hopeful, optimistic and sweet person . A post graduate in chemistry and on a regular mundane job she stumbled on books by accident and is still stuck there with them never wanting to come out it.
Reading fantasy, weaving stories in her head she made words her armour, pen her sword and books her trusted allies after that she never lost battles atleast not yet .
Hoping to pen her thoughts and read books in after life too."

Getting Old

I look at people getting old ,
And I realise the lines on their faces, the white colour of their hair and eyes
Eyes that could tell a lots of tales
From which we can learn and flourish "

Like A River

Soothing when calm , cruel when out of control
But having one goal to get into the ocean and complete the journey of falling into abyss and calmness ocean holds , to embrace someone by loosing identity and become one with ocean, to love someone like that
Like a river , beautiful on surface but witha lot of depth

Withered Relations

Mom I will balance my work and love life""!!.
All I am asking is don't be like your father"" .
He looked at his mother, "" why didn't you leave ?, for me maa!!
""No because i had hope that someday he will turn into that charming lover and adorable father, i managed to fall in love with. I didn't leave him for hope and now I have lost it and just like him I lost myself ""!!
The father was listening with an expensive gift in his hand only reminiscing, his woman liked fresh flowers more .
""So mom you are against his success""!!. His mother's smile was sad and wistful , ""I love him with his flaw but I will never be a part of his passion and he is ashamed of me , he loves me I know but I wish he was proud of me ""..
Her husband felt what he killed for non significant things and now that was irreplaceable, as she moved out of his room they both had tears in their eyes , as if mourning for their love. "

Smruti Paik

She is a girl who loves freedom and want everyone to experience it to the fullest. She strongly believes imagination and thoughts can do miracle. She loves nature thus pursuing her graduation as an Agricultural student. She is passionate, dynamic, imaginative & a dreamer . She loves connecting people whether through her artworks or through her writings.

Peeping Through The Window

Muddled in my own thoughts
in between the four walls,
it seemed like venture
but ultimately I lost somewhere
whether in my own thoughts or with my work,
I stopped peeping out
where my actual intrest was.

One summer day morning
near my window stool,
I heard creeping sound;
there was a Bluebird
not a prodigy but full of enthusiasm,
I was startled 'cause never seen before,
Bluebird sings it's song
as if wanted to imbue some thought.
Days passed and even months
this little bird now had brought spring indoors.

After someday the Bluebird lost somewhere
and I searched her everywhere,
downhearted me came near the window stool
peeped outside and saw a beautiful world,
Got my path of life to walk
the little bluebird showed me proper path!
Out of four walls began to fly in the limitless sky!

Himani Raheja

"Himani, she is a very wonderful person. She has a great talent of using words in different styles and techniques to deliver her ideas. All the poetries or writing work done by her is really very amazing. Her writings attract the readers and force them to wish to get her next work soon.

I wish very all the best to Himani for the future creations."

Insta id himaniraheja123.

अपने सपने

अनुभव है गहरा
इस ज़िंदगी में मेरा
चलना तो पड़ेगा ही
भले गिर जाओ मगर
उठना तो पड़ेगा ही ।।

हर नई सुबह उठकर,
विश्वास तो मन में
लाना पड़ेगा ही ।
पा लेंगे आज,
उन मंजिलों को हम
रह गए सपने जिसके
अधूरे कल कहीं ।।

ख़ुद को तो समझाना
होगा ही।
हौंसला तो अपना
बढ़ाना होगा ही ।
भले ही थोड़ी कठिन हैं,
ये राहें मगर ।
आगे तो इन पर
बढ़ना होगा ही।।

जीतेंगे ज़रूर
समझना ये होगा ही।
होंगे इक दिन सपने
अपने भी पूरे

भरोसा ये रखना होगा ही।।

हो जाएगी हर मुश्किल आसान
आगे बढ़ते जाएं जब हम
ढ़लने से पहले सूरज के
अपनी लगन कोशिशों के साथ
सफलता को पा लेंगे हम।।
सफलता को पा लेंगे हम।।

Ishita Kesarwani

Ishita Kesarwani is from prayagraj.She has just started writing poems and shayaris .She writes very nicely

मुस्कान

ज़िंदगी की सारी मुश्किलों से लड़ने के लिय मुझे बस एक चीज़ चाहिए... तुम्हारी सी मुस्कान ।

ज़िंदगी का हिस्सा

खूबसूरत सा एक पल क़िस्सा बन जाता है,
जाने कब कान ज़िंदगी का हिस्सा बन जाता है,
कुछ लोग ज़िंदगी में मिलते है ऐसे,
जिनसे कभी ना टूटने वाला रिश्ता बन जाता है ।

मंज़िल

मंज़िल इंसान के हौसले आज़माती है,
सपनो के पारदे आँखो से हटती है,
किसी बात से हिम्मत मत हारना,
ठोकर ही इंसान को चलना सीखतीं है ।
"

Jagdish

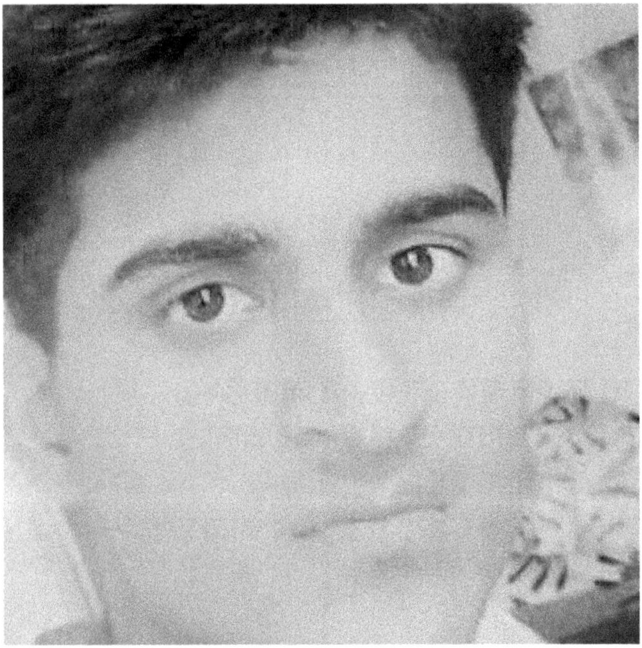

He is a good and great guy. He has very unique thinking and different dimensional point of view

अब क्या बताए की किस हाल में हैं

अब क्या बताए की किस हाल में हैं,
ठहर गए हैं दिन जिसके ऐसे एक साल में हैं।
रंग सारे देख चुका है मन, इस अतरंगी दुनिया के,
पर अभी भी मन मेरा गुम इसी के ख्याल में हैं।
फ़िक्र कर रहा हूं, उन रूठे यार-दोस्तों की,
हा, पता है मुझे छुपा खंजर उनकी ढाल में हैं।

कर ली दोस्ती नदामत में, अंदाजा था नहीं मुझे,
एक भेड़िया छुपा हिरन की खाल में हैं।

यू पहले बात बात पे झगड़ता तो नहीं था मैं,
तलाश सुकून की मुझे अब हर नए बवाल में हैं।अब क्या बताए

ऐ ज़िन्दगी तुझसे अब मेरा मन भर गया हैं।

मौत के आगोश में सो जाने दे मुझे अब
ऐ ज़िन्दगी तुझसे अब मेरा मन भर गया हैं।

मैं कर रहा था गीला खुद से आईने में,
एक उबाल आया ज़हन में मेरे, और अब कमरे में कांच बिखर गया हैं।

वो काफ़िला जो शरीक हुआ था मेरे उजले जमाने में,
इन अंधरो में डेरा उन जुगुनुओ का किधर गया हैं।

एक शख़्स रहता था मुझमें हंसता गाता मुस्कुराता,
दुख - दर्द के गहरे दरिये में डूब के मर गया है।

मौत के आगोश में सो जाने दे मुझे अब
ऐ ज़िन्दगी तुझसे अब मेरा मन भर गया हैं।

अब तक के सफर में,

कई लोग मिले है,
साथ है कुछ, कुछ बिछड़ गए उसी डगर में

सोचता हूं, कभी जाके हर एक के पास,
सवाल करू, मैं बुरा क्युं हूं उनकी नजर में

अब तो आदत में शुमार हैं बेवजह हंसना,
कहां लिखी हैं खुशियां मेरे मुकदर में

दिन गुजारता हूं, पत्थर समंदर में फेक फेक कर
रात को भी ठहर पाता नहीं हु मैं घर में

ऐ ज़िन्दगी, अब तो बातें कर लें खुलके मुझ तन्हा से ,
बोहत वक़्त जाया किया हैं तूने, अगर मगर में

Utkarsha Bhosale

"Utkarsha Bhosale,24, is a curious and over thinker girl from Nashik. she's professionally a Set Designer and was working in Indian film industry (Mumbai) as an Ass.Art Director.now she's trying to develop her ability of writing.she has a sensitive mind to record and observe little things and events in life.she loves to express her thoughts in poetic language.she is a Artist Sketcher Origami and Wanderlust person.recently she's working as a small event planner.
You can connect with her on utkarshabh80@gmail.com or @urkarsha014 on Instagram."

एक पल जिंदगी का

जिंदगी एक एहसास सुनकर लगता है, कुछ गहरा होगा. पर मुझे लगता है,जिंदगी का एहसास छोटे छोटे लम्हों मे छुपा हुआ है,जिस भी वक्त मेरे दिल को मेरे जिंदा होने का और मेरे वजुद का एहसास हो, वही तो एहसास- ए- जिंदगी है, जिंदगी में किसी भी खुबसुरत लम्हे का पहली बार मिला हुआ एहसास हमारे लिये हमेशा खास होता है. जैसे पहली बार किसी से महोब्बत होने का एहसास, पहली बार कुछ नया करने का एहसास, औरत का पहिली बार मां होने का एहसास,अपने नवजात बच्चे को गोद मे लेते ही एक आदमी को बाप होने का एहसास, मां बाप का सहारा बनते ही एक जिम्मेदार बेटा या बेटी होने का एहसास,एक बच्चे का स्कूल या कॉलेज का पहला दिन, पहला दोस्त,पहला प्यार, पहली नोकरी,पहली तनखा और वो हर पहली चीज जो खास हो.लेकीन फिर भी हमारी रोजमर्रा की जिंदगी मे भी हम कई अनोखे एहसासो से गुजरते है पर कभी गौर नही करते.बस हमारा उन्हे पहचानना जरुरी है,फिर ये आम सी जिंदगी भी खास लगने लगती है.

जिंदगी के सफर में हम कई अजनबी लोगों से मिलते है और कई अजीब अनुभवों का सामना करते है.इनमे से कुछ हमारे दिल को छु लेते है, कुछ हमे सिख दे जाते है तो कुछ हमे पुरी तरह से बदल देते है.ऐसा ही एक दिल छू लेने वाला वाक्या मेरे साथ भी हुआ.एक रोज की बात है,मै अपनी दोस्त के साथ अंधेरी पश्चिम के स्टेशन पर थी तभी मैने देखा, एक आदमी एस्कलेटर के पास बहोत देर से खडा है, और कुछ घबराया लग रहा है. मैने उनके पास जाकर देखा तो करीब ५५ तक उम्र होगी, गौर से देखा तो पता चला उनके हाथ भी काप रहे थे.मैने पूछा क्या बात है? आप कुछ डरे से लग रहे है,ऊस पर जवाब देते हुए उन्होंने कहा मुझे ऊपर जाना है,मैने कहा तो हर्ज ही क्या है.फिर वो बोले मुझे इन चलने वाली सिडीयो से डर लगता है, मै

गांव से आया हु, इस शहरं मे मेरी बेटी का ससुराल है,उसिसे मिलने आया था.मैने कहा अकेले आये है? उसपर वो बोले नही वो उपर बेटी और दामाद खडे है.मैने ऊपर देखा, उनकी बेटी ऊपर से आवाज लगा रही थी,""याना लवकर किती घाबरता तुम्ही"".

मैने उनका कापता हुआ हाथ अपने हाथों मे लिया और कहा डरने वाली कोई बात नही, जैसे ही एक सीडी खत्म हो दुसरी लगते ही पैर रख देना आईए हम साथ चलते है,उन्होंने ठीक वैसा ही किया,और हम ऊपर जाने लगे. मैने देखा वो थोडे भावूक हो गये थे और कहने लगे आसान था,पर मेरी बेटी कुछ सिखती ही नही, शायद मुझसे शरमिंदा हो जाती है, इसलिये मुझे अकेला छोड गयी.तुम जैसी होती तो मैं भी जमाने के साथ चलना सिख जाता,""तुम बहोत अच्छि बेटी बनोगी"".और जाते जाते मेरे सर पर हाथ रख के चले गये.मुझे अजीब लगा बच्चे मां बाप को रास्ते मे अकेला लडखडाता कैसे छोड सकते है.आखिर आज आप इस मॉडर्न जमाने के साथ चल सकते है तो इसकी वजाह भी तो वही है.जिन हाथों को पकड कर चलना सिखा आज उसिको भीड मे अकेला छोड दिया.हम सब भविष्य में जो कुछ भी बनते है उसके लायक तो हमे मां बाप ही बनाते है,फिर उनसे किस बात की शरमिंदगी.ये जिंदगी उन्हीं की बदौलत है और अगर मां बाप से ही शरमिंदा होना पडे तो वो जिंदगी ही क्या?

खैर छोडिये पर इस किस्से ने मुझे अनजाने मे बहोत कुछ सीखा दिया, मुझे अच्छा लगा की मै उनके काम आ सकी और मुझे लगा की मुझे भी अपने मम्मी पापा को बहोत सी नई चिजे सिखानी चाहिए, मुझे एहसास हुआ की शायद मे अच्छी बेटी और एक अच्छी इन्सान बन सकती हुं.

ये एक छोटा सा किस्सा था जो मेरे दिल को छू गया आखिर ऐसे ही छोटे छोटे किस्से ही तो हमारी जिंदगी के बेहतरीन हिस्से होते है.

मुझे लगता है हमारी जिंदगी एक बडी सी लायब्ररी की तरह है.जिसमे हमारे अलग अलग अनुभवो की,विविध घटनाओ की, एहसासो की, गिरणे उठणे की,हारणे जितने की और मर्मो की कहानियों की किताबे है.जब कभी जिस लम्हे की याद आ जाये तब बस किताब खोले और घंटो उसमे गुम हो जाए !!"

Asha Paul

आशा पॉल हिंदी तथा एजुकेशन में M.A. करने के पश्चात अध्यापन कार्य से जुड़ी हुई हैं ।

बचपन से ही कविताओं का इन्हें बहुत शौक था। 'रामधारी सिंह दिनकर' और 'महादेवी वर्मा' के साथ-साथ 'सुमित्रानंदन जी' की कविताएं इन्हें बहुत भाती थी। प्रकृति की कविताएं इन्हें बहुत ही मन को आकर्षित करने वाली लगती हैं और एक सुकून भी प्रदान करती हैं। धीरे ये भी कविता लिखने लगी और कविताओं से ही मन के भावों को सभी के समक्ष प्रस्तुत करने का इन्हें बहुत अच्छा जरिया दिखाई पड़ा।

समाज की विषमताओं के साथ-साथ हर तरह की भावनाओं को कविता द्वारा प्रस्तुत करने में एक अपना ही मजा है।"

खंडहर दिल

दिल खंडहर हो गया है। जब से एहसास नहीं कि तुम मेरे पास नहीं।
तुम्ही तो थे! जिसके साथ हंसती-बोलती थी।
तुम्ही तो थे !जिसकी कमी खलती थी।
तुम्ही तो थे! जो छुपा लिया करते थे अपनी पलकों में मुझे।
दुनिया से दूर बहुत दूर तुम्हारा जाना और मेरा हो जाना मज़बूर।
खंडहर हो गया अब ये मेरा मन न इसमें कोई रौनक न ही कोई उमंग।
काफिले ख़ुशियों के धुंधला चुके है। नज़र अब देखती है जाले जो लगे है,
मेरे चारों तरफ की तन्हाई में। मेरे एहसास न जाने क्यों उभरते ही नहीं।
मेरे मन को कुछ भाता ही नहीं। बस निस्तब्ध-सी ख़ामोशी सी है।
तुम्हारा मन नहीं होता ? आकर एक बार बस मेरे मन झांक कर देखने का।
कितनी धूल सी जैम गई है इस बेखौफ खंडहर में।
डराने लगी है लोगों को। वो अब मेरे पास आने से डरते है
और मैं हूँ कि उनके पास जाना ही नहीं चाहती।
तुम क्यों नहीं समझते मुझे मेरी मजबूरियों को ?
मेरे बीते समय को न सही आने वाले हर घड़ी को लौटा दो।
मेरे वीरान खंडहर को फिर से एक बार घर बना दो।
न मरना मेरे नसीब में न जीना मेरे हाथ में।
तुम्हारी तलब में प्यासी सी बैठी हूँ बस इंतज़ार में।
कोई तो तरकीब होगी ? कही तो मेरी भी मंजिल होगी।
तुम जो चाहो तो सहर होगी।
तुम जो चाहो तो सहर होगी। "

बदलती दुनिया, बदलते लोग

किस ने सोचा था। 'कोरोना' आएगा।
देखते ही देखते सब बदल जायेगा।
नौकरी, पढ़ाई, रिश्ते सब पर कहर ढायेगा।
किसे पता था सब बदल जायेगा?
ऊँचे मीनारों पर या झोपड़ी मकानों में,
घरों, दुकान या कि कारखानों में, सभी जगह; एक ही, हाल है।
हर कोई, इसकी मार से बेहाल है।
तुम्हें तो पता होगा, कैसा ये माहौल है?
सूझता नहीं क्या करें ? कब तक ऐसा ही रहेगा ये दौर है?
बहुत कुछ बदल गया और बदल रहा अभी।
वो शामें न रही, वो मंजर न रहा।
कितनों का घर लूटा, कितनों ने लगाई फांसी।
कितनों की रोजी बंद, कितनों नहीं शुकुन जरा-सी।
वो ख़ुशी, वो हंसी, वो चहकना न रहा।
वो बच्चे, वो स्कूल, वो लहकना न रहा।
कितना ही रोको; बार-बार ख्याल को,
मानता नहीं ये मन कि अब वो 'मस्त मन' न रहा।
मिलना-जुलना हाल बांटना, वो खिलखिलाना न रहा।
मूवी जाना, मिलना-मिलाना, Get-together न रहा।
मन है भारी जेब हल्की, दोस्ताना न रहा।
तुम तो सुन लो। बात मेरी, मेरा जिगरी न रहा।
खिलखिलाकर, मुस्कुराती, रूठती और मानती।
गलियों से गुजरती, वो नजारा न रहा।
क्या-क्या भुला दूँ ? मेरी खुशियों का, एक भी ठिकाना
अब तो बाकी न रहा।
थोड़ा-सा जो अब बचा है; वो न मुझसे छीनना।

मेरा लिखना और पढ़ना या की तुमसे बात करना।
ये ही बाकी अब रहा।
ये ही बाकी अब रहा।"

इबादत

बड़े चाव से दोस्त बनाया, खुदा बन गए।
इबादत उसकी जगह तेरी करने लगे ।
इबादत उसकी जगह तेरी करने लगे ।
अब वो हाल है कि अपनी ही दुआओं से डरने लगे

www.ingramcontent.com/pod-product-compliance
Lightning Source LLC
Chambersburg PA
CBHW050520240926
51846CB00003B/638
* 9 7 8 9 3 9 0 4 1 6 2 6 4 *